I0700053

Altered State of Affairs

BY JERALD KASIMOV

This book is a work of fiction. Names, characters, places, and incidents are the product of the author's imagination or are used fictitiously. Any resemblance to actual events, locales, or persons, living or dead, is coincidental.

Copyright © 2022 by Jerald Kasimov
jeraldkasimov.com

Cover design by Terri Katz Kasimov, Cooper Kasimov, and Bill Nimelman

All rights reserved. No part of this book may be reproduced, scanned, or distributed in any printed or electronic form without permission. Please do not participate in or encourage piracy of copyrighted materials in violation of the author's rights.

All trademarks, service marks, and company names are the property of their respective owners.

Produced and published by:
KazSource, Inc
kazsource.com

November 2022

ISBN: 979-8-9868008-0-6

DEDICATION

To my family: L'dor v'dor. From generation to generation... Blessed to be of you and with you always and forever.

ACKNOWLEDGEMENTS

Many thanks to Austin Roberts, Caroline Ailanthus, and Mary Lib Morgan, my editors and mentors who taught me what it takes to be a writer.

To my wife, eternal soulmate and influencer, Terri Katz Kasimov. Thank you for your passion, encouragement, and unqualified belief in me.

Most especially, to one of my two extraordinary sons, Eric Kasimov, publisher, entrepreneur, and disrupter. Thank you for your energy, courage, expertise, and vision to make this book happen. You continue to blow me away! Special kudos to your exceptional team at KazSource including Shane Snively and Scott Upton who helped pave the way for this incredible journey.

My heart is full.

PROLOGUE

Heroes are ordinary people who make themselves
extraordinary.
— *Gerard Way*

Dawn is breaking; it's a beautiful morn. The sky, a bright azure, the air crisp—allowing nature's dew to rejuvenate the thirsty foliage and elicit the therapeutic jasmine aroma. How do I know that condensation increases as the dew point decreases? Well, after taking a John Carroll University physics class with Professor Sister Shelley, I became an expert on condensation, but that's a whole other story.

Avra and I hike up the mountain to the nearest ledge. It offers a 180° vista of the magnificent plain below—the River L'Ariège meandering through the foothills of the great Pyrenees, proudly reflecting the steadfast rising sun. You can see forever.

Off to the side are the remarkable remnants of an ancient cave, fortified over the years with an array of huge multi-colored stones and seemingly decorated by our creator with intermingling verdant grass, moss, and ferns.

What a glorious day this will be with the mist climbing from the valley and the sunshine beginning to bathe the lush vegetation with its warmth. Embracing our mystical surroundings, however, would be pathetically futile as we are on a critical mission to save the world from a horrifying weapon of mass destruction. Time is running out. There are only a few more grains of sand left in the hourglass.

Girls don't understand that peeing is an art form but relieving myself in this majestic setting was spiritual. What a perfect place to piss. Trying to rush just makes it more difficult.

"Hurry the fuck up," Avra orders.

Finally, shaking off the last drop, I hear footsteps. I turn to see two frickin' terrorists aiming AK-47s at Avra's head.

Chapter 1

The year 2006 was a very good one; very good indeed. Saddam Hussein was killed, and I want to snuff the next crazy jihadist and all his asshole friends. Terrorists, or destructionists, as they prefer to be called, are no longer satisfied with destroying a bus, a plane, two enormous buildings, or gassing six million people. They now want to obliterate cities, destroy continents, or even eradicate humanity. They are obtaining the tools. My name is Steven and this is where I come in.

Before whacking the bad guys, completing Ranger training is my first hurdle. After graduating from The Ohio State University ROTC program with a master's degree in electrical engineering, I enlist in the army. This is not a rash decision. My lifelong dream has been to be a Delta Force guy with a focus on black ops, a unit which technically doesn't exist—except everyone knows it does, like baseball pitchers don't use 'stuff' on their fingers. Get my drift? Exactly.

The process is extremely difficult, but I am determined to ultimately be selected by the revered fraternity known as Delta Force, and Army Rangers are my entrée to this sacred world. However, you have to be extraordinarily qualified and sail through the agonizingly difficult training levels to even be considered for Delta. In addition, four years of special ops service is a demanding prerequisite. Hard to believe, but I have all the makings to be this improbable soldier.

A critical component of Ranger matriculation is paratroop expertise. To attain that level, graduation from the Army Airborne School in Fort Benning is mandatory. Unfortunately, an extreme emphasis is placed on jumping. No shit. Now, free falling over water, landing in barely survivable conditions like snake-infested swamps, and night deployment are not on my bucket list. They also practice water survival techniques from a simulated downed aircraft, trapping us in the famous 'helo dunker.' Brutal.

The weight training facility at the jump school is on par with that of any NFL or major college football team. Every piece of equipment imaginable—from free weights and bench presses to exotic Cybex machines and treadmills galore—all for our use. You name it; they have it. After all, only the best for Ranger School. This is where I hang in my spare time—working out like crazy and schmoozing with my fellow trainees.

...*love* going through my bench press routine, like in high school with that asshole, Coach Kilgore, screaming in my ear. I can still hear him ranting, "Push harder! Push, you son-of-a-bitch!"

Then one day, this strange dude Jabber just shows up at the workout area unannounced. He parks himself on the adjacent weight bench and tells me straight up that he's my new best friend—self-appointed, I guess. Never met him before. This red-headed, curly-haired, wiry kid clings to me like a wet T-shirt, always there, never leaving my side. We hit it off immediately. It's a mutually beneficial relationship—I crave his joviality and confidence, and he needs my credibility.

After pressing the heavies with AC/DC blasting, trying to outperform each other, we move to squats. I always beat him. Eternally competitive, I refuse to lose. My mother always told me that I was a genius, but that I needed to apply myself. Unfortunately, she had me tested and, as predicted, I scored off the charts in every conceivable brain check. So now there was no excuse. She nagged me incessantly to apply myself. Unfortunately, I was born into a family of super-achievers.

Mom was brilliant: Phi Beta Kappa, president of Mortar Board, and voted most-outstanding woman at Ohio University. Her older brother, Max, deaf and speechless, graduated from Case Western Reserve School of Engineering, where he played tight end on their football team. So, when my mom told me I was under-performing, she definitely had street cred. Another brother, Bill, a graduate of The Ohio State University Medical School, was a famous hand surgeon. This was a tough act to follow. So, when I wasn't the best, there was hell to pay.

I didn't like to be told what to do—wanted to be my own boss. This further corroborated the obsession to self-determine my destiny. I was a risk-taker who lived on the edge, always yearning for that adrenaline rush, magical endorphins—those legal drugs produced by your body that help you accomplish great things. They are frickin' addicting.

That's what I crave on a daily basis—to kick ass, get ass, and feel great. What I really need is to please myself—to honestly satisfy that untamed guy in the mirror and say, "I tried my hardest, motherfucker—did my best." Sometimes it isn't enough. Keep pounding, asshole.

Finishing the workout with a 10-mile run on the treadmill, Jabber yells, "Hey Stevie, "Where ya from?" Before I can even answer he declares, "I'm from here," with his deep southern accent. "The glorious rural Georgia Lowcountry, nice huh? Daddy took off when I was a little kid; there's some guy running around out there with red hair. Must be my father, haha. Mama raised me and taught me how to take care of myself. Little brother is in the Navy; don't see him much. Three older sisters ran away with guys—whatever. Haven't heard hide nor hair since. Mama keeps in touch with 'em, but I don't give a shit. You're going to be my new brother."

"Sure, okay," I say. "My real little brother, ah—we're not very close either—hardly ever see him. Jabber, ya know what? I could use a brother." Sigh. "So, do you remember your father?" I ask.

"Sort of, red hair and all that," he responds, vaguely. "Never really had a job… just worked on his radio a lot in the basement."

"Doin' what?" I ask.

"Dunno, just fiddling around, I guess, talking gibberish to

people who also talked gibberish. Mama told me he liked staying in touch with friends from the old country. Then one day, he just took off. Never freaking saw him again, that son of a bitch," Jabber hisses.

"Where were your parents from originally?" I ask, thinking about his father talking strangely to folks from afar.

"Didn't really speak much about it—I know, pretty weird, huh?" he asks, shrugging his shoulders. Jabber continues before I can say anything else. "Hey Steve, whatcha doin' for New Year's Eve? Would love to watch the fireworks over the Mediterranean. Supposed to be cool and all that. Wanna go with me?"

"Jabber, it's eight months away!"

"Simmer down. Just so excited. Love the blues and reds and especially the loud noises—like bombs going off. Makes your bones shake. Stevie, you're going with me. We'll have so much fun."

I remember from chemistry that minerals are the color source for fireworks. Copper produces blue; sodium yields yellow; while strontium makes the reds. Every color in the rainbow can be produced with variations and mixtures of natural substances from the earth. Master fireworks makers are like artists using their palettes to generate spectacularly vivid creations. It could be a future vocation for Jabber, but he would probably blow himself up.

"Ok, we'll see," I agree. "Can't plan that far ahead. Just focus on our training for now, alright, Jabber?"

Ignoring me, he just keeps talking. "Well, we can always go on a picnic and eat some Italian sausage sandwiches. If that doesn't sound appetizing, we could just go to one of the bars and listen to some live music. Doesn't have to be New Year's; it can be any day."

"Jabber, you are really something. Your lips move faster than your brain," I chuckle.

"C'mon Stevie, be nice. Found a good buddy and you're already trying to dump me," he scolds.

"That's not true… just tone it down a little," I say.

"Oh, all right, it's just my way. Hey Steven, you're a fearless SOB—can see it in your eyes. Goin' to fly right through training and show these dudes. Gonna be stars, All Pros, watch us. Betcha I could teach these guys. Pay attention to me, ok? Won't let you down," he tells me.

"Jabber, don't be so cocky," I caution.

"Whaddaya talkin'... cocky? Called confident. Just hang with me. Goin' to get you through this shit with flying colors. You're my guy, Steven."

"Jabs, you talk too much," I point out. "Never let me reply. I'm from Cleveland. Went to Cleveland Heights High School and The Ohio State University. Broke some hearts and got some good hand jobs. Caused some mischief on the way, like shooting up Freddy's pool room with some pellet guns, ya know... stuff like that."

"Cool! ...never been to Cleveland," he says, "but did go to Michigan with a full ride football scholarship. I'm a Wolverine."

"No wonder. That's your problem; Buckeyes eat Wolverines. You must've been pretty bad to get a scholarship to that school up north," I laugh.

"Yeah, whatever. How are you feeling?" he asks.

"Nervous, really scared about the training exercises coming up, like I'm gonna barf. Been hearing horror stories, dudes talking trash. Man, don't know if I can cut it. Hell, there are rumors about people getting hurt or worse. The dropout rate is supposed to be ridiculous—guys quitting in the middle of drills," I rant on.

"Bullshit, you da man, Stevie, a born killer. You'll see... tomorrow's supposed to be great weather for jumping out of planes. Gonna make your mama proud," Jabber says as he fist bumps me.

Today is the tomorrow that you worried about
yesterday.
— Dale Carnegie

It's a beautiful April morning with the spectacular sunrise somewhere in the Upcountry of Georgia. Conditions couldn't have been better for a picnic or a hike in the woods, but that's not on our agenda. Our platoon leaders have something else in mind—parachuting. My greatest fear, other than failure, is fear of heights. Ultimately, we'll have to make hundreds of jumps from all kinds of aircraft. Experience is key. Every type of nature's wrath: wind, rain, heat, cold, desert, and water, are required for training.

Climbing ladders, let alone jumping from airplanes with fifty pounds of gear, is not in my wheelhouse. They give us artificially weighted Molle 4000 rucksacks attached to our parachutes so the jumping exercises will simulate real time conditions. They tell us that the amazingly versatile waterproof packs are designed to maintain a lower center of gravity by distributing the weight from the shoulders to the hips. This allows for better balance and airflow, they explain.

The Molle packs can carry just about anything, depending on the mission: food rations, sleeping bag, extra pistol of choice—usually an M9 Beretta, ammo, gun cleaning kit, first aid stuff, drinking water bladder, flashlight, night vision gear, incendiary grenades, and different types of explosives—whatever is necessary.

Instructors prime us for every conceivable situation. We practice our skill sets in the classroom, then move on to safety-assisted tower jumping, and finally get to the real deal—parachuting at 1200 feet from a fixed wing aircraft. Not much room for error. At least the first few jumps utilize a static line to engage the rip cord. After that— all bets are off—we're on our own. This is just the beginning for every Special Forces unit. Further training is compulsory to hone our talents in every imaginable operation, under the most extreme duress.

"Going to be a piece of cake," I mumble to everyone, trying to psych myself up. No one's listening. All nervous wrecks, except Jabber, who is babbling. The guys just stare. Nobody knows quite what to make of his eccentricities. He is a unique character—someone you'd remember forever.

"Jabber, time to rumble," I tell him. "Let's show these guys how it's done." I'm shaking in my boots.

"There you go, Stevie. That's my boy." He's always trying to pump me up, give me confidence—like my mom, but with a southern accent.

About twenty of my colleagues join us in a small, fixed-wing aircraft previously used in some desolate third-world country's war to quickly get in and out of compromised landing strips. It's now exclusively deployed for jump training at Fort Benning. The initial maneuver is going to be a simple operation: jump, land, rendezvous, pick up, and do it again three more times before lunch. So nauseated that eating is out of the question.

To make matters worse, another guy, who also has bright red curly hair, is already puking his brains out. Looks like Howdy Doody after eating a bad oyster from the marsh.

"That must be your twin brother over there. Maybe ya have the same father, eh?" I say to Jabber.

"Different mama, haha," he retorts.

After watching the other guy retch for a while, I turn to Jabber and grunt, "Fuck, gonna lose my guts. Seriously."

"Hey Stevie, you don't look so good. Relax, man. I'll pull you through this. Be tough. You can do it," he tells me emphatically.

This whole Ranger thing is getting to me; don't know if I can survive boot camp. Man, I'm fucking nauseated. Shit. Doesn't help that most of the other guys are sick. Wonder if this happens on every jump? Can't imagine doing this and then going into battle and getting shot at or worse. Jesus, what a way to make a living. I'm so fucking scared, but no quitting. Gonna get through this.

Looking down, I can see my hands shaking.

Shit. What the fuck was I thinking, wanting to be a Ranger—Delta Force no less? Oh man!

At least I have a friend here. He's such a weird son of a bitch, but he's certainly attached himself to me. There are a lot of other guys here; why me? Maybe 'cause I'm so likable.

"Trying, Jabs—I'm trying," I assure him, but not with much confidence.

"Fight your fears: fight 'em, fight 'em, fight 'em!" he shouts.

"Jabber, do you ever stop talking?" I ask, annoyed.

"No. Why should I? Just trying to help you, man," he replies, sounding miffed. "Would never hurt you, Stevie... right?"

Holy shit. Just met this guy—don't even know his real name—just appeared from nowhere and parked himself right next to me.

"Hey Jabs, never asked your real name in case I have to tell your mama you died. What is it?" I ask him seriously.

"James," he says proudly.

"James?"

"Yeah," he answers. "Little brother was just learning to talk, couldn't say James; called me Jabber. Stuck. Friends kidded me that I talked lots, so Jabber was perfect."

Looking around the plane, nobody seems very happy. Everybody's caught up in their own shit, with their own fears. Heads are down—not a real positive sign. This would not go over big with my coaches.

"Heads up, be confident, focus—get your brain in the game!" they would scream, and they were right.

The aircraft has no seats and no windows; everyone is sitting on the floor like they're ready to take a dump or puke. Straps and netting cover the walls and ceiling to help stabilize everybody and everything.

Need to get my mind off the jump and focus on something else... Maybe one of my hand jobs in high school:

Man, those were good times—free as a bird. President of BAT, short for Beta Alpha Tau, that prodigious high school fraternity—been around for almost 100 years. Great traditions and kids who would become masters of the universe in their professions: college presidents, doctors, businessmen, lawyers, professors, and now me— Steven, the Army Ranger Delta Force wannabe. Priceless memories.

We were naughty but not juvenile delinquents—merely cool badasses. The best looking, smartest, and finest athletes... We ruled: president of the school, stars of the football, baseball, and basketball teams but we were really depraved. College scholarships and great futures awaited but an occasional night in jail made us more well-rounded. We were not criminals, just broke a few windows or engaged in some sporadic drunken orgies. Blowing up the principal's mailbox with a cherry bomb or breaking the nose of someone who would dare challenge one of us seemed like harmless fun and reasonable things to do. We were so nasty that girls loved us, and other guys despised us.

That's the way it should be. Their mothers adored us, and their fathers hated us. That's also the way it should be, and that's the way it was. I really don't think the fathers knew that we occasionally pulled out our dicks at parties. Their daughters would scream bloody murder and pretend not to look. Jonny was always the first. He would yell, "Dick is out!" That was the signal. If the fathers only knew that these were the same kids they cheered for at the Friday night football games. Nancy, one of our cutest classmates, would usually scream the loudest and run away shrieking, "Disgusting!" She also gave great hand jobs.

Being president of our infamous organization gave me a lot of pride as well as a great deal of responsibility. I was usually the one called into the office to explain why Jonny drove his "Indian" motorcycle down the long front hall of the school yelling "Fuck!" or why Victor mooned the assistant principal in the parking lot. These things were hard to explain. They were spontaneous. They just happened. Now you've got to understand—back then there were no drugs. HIV had not been discovered. Kids did not kill kids. We did not have weapons. "Zero tolerance" had not yet been coined. We were bad, but the school put up with us. So, one of my jobs as the prez was to put out fires and keep my brilliant brothers in school so that their budding careers in medicine, law, and business would be fulfilled. Had to keep their permanent records clean. It wasn't easy, but it was my sacred responsibility—almost like black ops.

Back to reality: "Jabs, you're growing on me. Keep talking," I tell him. It's taking my mind off this crazy Ranger shit—jumping out of planes and whatever else they throw at us."

"Yessiree Stevie, my boy," he answers with glee.

Interesting that Jabber has not befriended anyone else. Never even speaks to the other guys; maybe just one of his quirks. Good guy though. It's nice having a buddy to go through this stuff with.

Suddenly, the jump zone alert blares with flashing yellow lights and a probing foghorn sequence: *On deck. On deck. On deck.*

"Oh, shit," I mumble.

Harsh, penetrating lights violate my eyes. Deafening sounds reverberate through my ear drums. Spasms of pain rock my body. In other words, I am fucked. Head exploding. Hyperventilating. Nauseous. Time stands still. All sounds become one; don't understand. Flashing lights everywhere. Paralyzed... it's my turn, but I can't move.

The CO screams, "Jump, you fucking asshole, or I'll shoot!"

Flapping like a fish out of water, I realize I am staring at the sun with my head up my ass, accelerating straight down to motherfucking Earth. Going to die! The chute finally deploys—a miracle—thanks to the static line. Stopped breathing. Catapulting ever so closer—trying to steer to the landing zone. Fighting to scream. Lungs on fire, can't inhale. Scream! Scream! Trying so hard. Straining to open my mouth, but it's locked.

Ground approaching. Total panic. Screaming. Howling like a newborn baby sliding down the infamous chute of life. All comes pouring out, a neurovascular reboot.

"Ahhhhhhhhhhhhhh!" I yell with all my innards trying to get

out. Could breathe, my body relaxes—flaccid, like a dead fish. Somersaults on the ground never felt this good. I am reborn.

Turning around, there's Jabber bellowing, "Good job, you motherfucker. We are BFFs. Let's go kill some terrorists."

"Damn straight. Let's do it! I can do this shit, James! Born killer. Gonna make it through training. Can't stop me now!"

Maybe Jabber showed up in my life to save me from myself.

"That's it, Stevie!" he yelps. "Gonna do it together, you and me, bud."

Surveying the area, I can see most of the other guys gathering in their chutes. Most look okay but one of the trainees, a nice kid from Missouri, is flat on his back, and the medics are working on him—not sure what's wrong. Don't want to know. Another guy, from Mississippi, limping badly, probably a sprained ankle. At least he's walking.

The plane has already landed close by, and we all quickly make our way back for another adrenaline producing jump. This one has to be better. I'm actually looking forward to it—once you accomplish something, you know you can do it again, only better—unless something bad happens.

Chapter 2

HELO DUNKER

The helo dunker is the most important of all survival training exercises. An adjunct to all types of water missions and rescues, it teaches us how to safely exit any type of submerged structure. The dunker is so critical in our training that two full days are dedicated to perfecting our skills. The exercise is a mind fucker that teaches us not to panic—easier said than done. Trust in our buddies is paramount as we train to gain confidence in our abilities to meet dangerous situations head on.

Prior to joining the Rangers, I asked some of my friends' older brothers to share their experiences with me. They said that the dunker was all mental. Physicality was not the issue; it was overcoming the psychology of fear. Right up my alley.

Our instructors demonstrate the techniques and show us what to do. We see a movie of an actual exercise, but doing it in real time will be quite different. I await the big day with vicious butterflies eating away at my stomach.

The helo is set up as part of a huge water training facility. Anything that has to do with water instruction can be taught, learned, and practiced here. All sorts of equipment are scattered throughout the giant indoor/outdoor building, including various types of diving gear—both pressurized deep-sea and scuba. An area where we could practice underwater welding and utilization of demolition equipment is attached in the rear. The place is extraordinary.

As we enter the space, the special crane that holds and controls the dunker is the first thing I notice. It looks like a giant praying mantis ready to eat its prey, hopefully not me. So fucking claustrophobic! All I can focus on is being locked up in that frickin' helo. The five-minutes-to-get-ready buzzer sounds. My heart is pounding in my throat. They tell us to enter the helo. When we are all positioned correctly, the instructor asks for our attention.

"Ok guys, sit there for a few minutes; take a few breaths," says the platoon leader. He's in here with us for safety reasons. "Try to imagine that you're on a rescue mission over the ocean and something happens. You go down. This is what you're gonna experience."

The crane drops us like a bird rejecting a fish—a gigantic *SPLASH* similar to the cannonball dive from when we were kids, only a thousand times bigger.

The helo violently rocks with the waves.

"Fuck."

The dunker sinks as the water replaces the air, then turns over upside down.

Panic hits.

Miraculously, I get myself under control. For the first time, I feel exhilaration from those magic endorphins. My helicopter mates and I share a few air tanks as we methodically unlatch the windows and get the fuck out of there.

On top of the water now, all nine of us are present. Thankfully nobody is missing. I raise my arms, "Whoooooeeeee! Love this shit."

The CO smiles, "Steven, you may even be a Ranger one fine day."

"Yes sir."

"We are ready to lead, Jabber!" I shout at the top of my lungs.

"Gonna be right next to you, my friend," as he lovingly rubs my head. "We're going to kick some ass," he declares for everyone to hear.

There is only one thing that makes a dream
impossible to achieve: the fear of failure.
— Paul Coelho, The Alchemist

There is more than a sixty percent attrition rate during Ranger training. Know why? Terror and fear of failure. Fear can be overpowering, even incapacitating. It's not what the Ranger command is looking for in a candidate. To be human is to have the ability to fear. To be a Ranger is to have the power and capacity to overcome the demons. Horror created by heights, water submersion, and personal injury can be astounding.

Initial Ranger Assessment School and subsequent specialist

training teaches the soldier to defeat panic. Anxiety is normal. Nature provides every species with the facility to fear their predator. Survival of the fittest is as old as life itself—Darwinism. Those that endure utilize fright as a means of survival.

"No" is not in my vocabulary. Second place is never good enough. The Rangers have a very willing and receptive participant, just have to overcome a few phobias. No way am I going to bomb out unless my brain fucks me up the ass.

That's the problem. It's me against my gray matter, but in the end, I will prevail. Always a helluva battle. Listen, I have some issues; everybody does. Mine are different—I must win. No alternative. Losing sucks. A gut-fucker. That's the deal. The torment of defeat is almost as bad as fear itself…sometimes worse. Failing is like dying. It sucks out your soul so there is nothing else for which to live. Failure rationalizations are a cop out. Sure, some days will be livable; but when you're all alone, that guy in the mirror will never forget. Will always remember you are one mother-fuckin-sorry asshole. That's what drives me. Never ever want that son-of-a-bitch scrutinizing, looking, peering, or hating me. Loathe that creature. That's why I refuse to fail. Never.

…had a lot of coaches in my day—some good, some bad. Most were concerned with just winning. A few, like Coach Kilgore, would paddle players if they screwed up or make them squat until they fell over. Not a good way to teach, but looking back, it was great preparation for the Rangers.

Jabs says, "You're a born winner, Stevie. If you take my advice, I'll coach you through this stuff. We'll practice our drills together. Gonna be so much fun. Jabber is at your service. I have many skills," he brags. "Can hunt squirrel, kill gators, make frog soup three different ways: spicy, creamy, or with a touch of strawberry marmalade."

Yikes, there he goes again. "What the fuck you talkin' about?" I ask.

"Anything you want, man. Girls, guys, or frogs. We're the best the Army has to offer, you and me, Stevie," he declares.

"Wha?"

What the hell is he ranting about? Guys? Frogs? Sometimes it's all mumbo jumbo. Jesus. Strange dude, but what the heck? I knew some wild motherfuckers in high school who could give Jabber a run for his money.

Chapter 3

WATER SURVIVAL TEST

They take us out, five at a time, by boat to a pontoon raft about three football fields out. We'll have to swim back to shore. Jabbar is right there next to me of course, singing, "Oh, what a beautiful morning," by Rodgers and Hammerstein.

A lovely spring sunrise... conditions are perfect for the combat water survival test, or CWST as it is called. The large man-made lake, like you see all over the south, probably originated from the Tennessee Valley Authority water development project in the '50s. Not sure if they have any alligators, but I'm afraid to ask. They do, however, have a wide variety of snakes, mostly non-venomous. Not sure I could tell the difference unless I got bit—then I'd know for sure.

Every candidate must become proficient in all environments and each component of the Earth's surface: air, land, and good ol' H_2O. I feel confident in passing the water training with relative ease. Always been a pretty good swimmer. I even participated in an Ironman event. Placed well.

"Hey, Jabs. What's up?"

"Hey man—we're going to the beach. Maybe we can get a little surfing in. C'mon Stevie; gonna have a ball. Better put on suntan lotion," he instructs.

"You're nuts," I tell him. *Gee, maybe he is crazy. It's like he's putting on a show for me.*

"It's how I get through the day, man. Gonna do this together, bud. You and me, Steven," he preaches.

"Right," I sigh.

"Let's go," Jabs says.

He's starting to get on my nerves; needs to tone it down a little. He means well, but…wow.

"C'mon Stevie, sing with me. C'mon."

Holy shit, the CO is gonna think we're off our rockers.

"You're crazy," I say. "Ok, ok."

"In unison, now!" he yells.

Oh, what a beautiful morning.

Things are great until they cover our eyes and order us to jump in the water with full gear and swim to shore. Fucking blindfolded— nobody bothered to tell me that part. Maybe it's a good thing, 'cause I would've taken the first bus out of here.

The artificially weighted rucksack is like the one we used with the jumps. For the real deal, Rangers would also carry the same kind of emergency provisions, MREs, M9 with extra ammo, underwater welding torches, and anything else that would be required for that particular mission, from explosives to rescue equipment. Everything would always be water-proofed and sealed in special plastic sacks. For some missions, we could carry inflatable rafts, change of clothing, anything that's mobile.

Being blindfolded is very claustrophobic—starting to panic. No fuckin' way. Blindfold has to stay on the whole way or else. Can't do it. I can still feel Coach Kilgore's paddle blackening my ass with huge welts that last for weeks. Shit, if I can do that, I can do this for sure. Fuck all of you bastards. Goin' to be a piece of cake.

Jabber starts screaming, "Yes, you can. Let's jump together and sing," and he grabs my hand. "Oh, what a beautiful morning!"

"Wait, wait a minute. Hold on. Gonna piss my pants!" I yell.

Just then two officers scream, "Jump, you fuckers," and push us into the lake. "Don't come back or we'll drown you," laughing at the top of their lungs.

Sound like fucking Kilgore, that piece of shit.

My body explodes. Shuts down. Loses control.

Foghorns blare, but there is no fog. Gasping for air. Going to fucking croak. Better than quitting. Don't want to die.

Please don't let me die here... under water. Choking. Pissing. Blindfolded. Swimming. Struggling. Oh man. Seems like eternity. Miles and miles to go. Shit!

Then... hearing the CO booming through the bullhorn, "You got it, soldier—only ten yards to go. Rip off the blindfold; you're home free!"

Bubbles. Can see bubbles.

Staring up to an incredibly blue sky, my spirit victorious. The commanding officer is cheering as I pull myself out of the water.

"Good work," he howls. "Fantastic, I knew you could do it!"

My world changes from Eric Church's 'Dark Side' to Sinatra's 'My Blue Heaven.' This is the feeling of exhilaration I so desperately need. Everything is clear and sweet—the endorphins exploding. I think there is a smile on my face, but I try not to laugh. My confidence level is definitely trending up.

"Fuckin' A, dude," Jabber bellows out. "You da man."

"You assholes are like an old married couple, ha!" the CO laughs. "Wait till you do the live fire drill; gonna shit your drawers."

Chapter 4

LIVE FIRE

Live fire blasting—monstrously powerful M240L machine guns begin their onslaught. Tracer rounds flying everywhere, creepily lighting up the muck, creating a line-of-sight trajectory to aid in re-calibration of the weapons. The flashes are small, pyrotechnic charges fired from those same guns—every fifth or sixth shot lights up. Can see gator eyes staring us down. Gotta crawl over this shit and get to those trees over there. Between here and there is the problem, the makings of a horror film.

NOT a beautiful morning in Georgia. This time, a miserable night in a Lowcountry backwater swamp with a cold mist full of gators galore and prehistoric sounds. Piercing screams from things being eaten; warnings from critters, large and small, protecting their territory. It's a classic turf war—survival of the fittest—Darwinism at its best. Coral snakes and water moccasins slither between our boots. Spooky.

"Hey Stevie!" Jabs yells. "Keep your fucking head down. It's showtime—haha."

"Yeah man, you get hit in the head; your red hair will be charcoal black," I warn him.

There are explosions everywhere as the deadly rounds smash into the cypress trees, then ricochet in all directions. Wood and bark disintegrate. Imagine what these 7.62 mm bullets could do to a human body. Don't want to know! Fuckin' A.

My bones vibrate; everything's ablaze. The essence of gunpowder permeates the air. The real lesson of battle: every time someone moves, they fire rounds that miss us by inches. Hopefully these fuckers know it's a training exercise, but it is well documented that accidents do happen.

"Stevie, gonna shit my pants if those bullets get any closer. Fuck, think I did. Something smells awful," Jabs complains.

"Swamp gas, asshole. You should know that. Y'all from heya," imitating Jabber's accent. "Everything stinks in the swamp. Methane bubbling up. Clears your sinuses," I explain.

"Yikes, too close for comfort. You think they realize we're on a high-crawl drill, not a low-crawl?" Jabs asks.

"Good question, but too late to ask; just keep your head down. Maybe you should take off your helmet so they can see your red hair," I kid.

"They'll think I'm a wild turkey and then shoot me for sure," he screams over the ear-splitting noise.

Disgustingly soggy, we have to maneuver under the fire line

across the bog to the free zone, about a football field away. That's our destination—we'll pass the test and not get killed. Besides all the critters trying to eat us, there are stretches of soft sucking mud, like quicksand, that would be a slow death or worse. Leading the way as we move forward, it's my job to probe the depths with a long pole to determine areas of deadly gunk that could suck us in for eternity.

We've been warned to avoid sections where there's no water. Pluff mud lurks there. Too late. My left foot sinks—feels like the suction will rip the boot off. I can't move, too afraid to put my right foot down. Panic sets in. Fuck! "Help!" I scream. "Help me, Jabber! I'm stuck!"

Being drawn down, now mud up to my waist, my right foot also trapped—feel myself sinking deeper. Holy shit.

"Jabs, fucking help me. Can't move, no traction... going down! Help!" I shriek at the top of my lungs. "Please hurry!"

Georgia swamps suck! Fucking miserable day and getting worse. Now raining heavily. Can't see shit!

Suddenly Jabber appears.

"What's the problem, big fella?" he's asking me like he's totally oblivious, seemingly unconcerned.

"I can't move! Get me the fuck out of here. Grab the pole," I order.

Jabber, standing in a stable spot, grabs the end of the metal rod and tries pulling in his direction. Nothing. No traction. Won't budge. Can't risk falling into the sink hole with me. If it keeps raining, I'm fucked. It's very apparent that somehow I need to get hoisted vertically and still avoid the live rounds.

"Help me Jabs—getting sucked in more," I beg. "Please!"

A vulture flies by, sensing trouble and maybe an opportunity for dinner. I glance up as the bird of prey whisks away to tell his friends. As if on cue, he returns to perch on a massive oak branch right above us; we could use it for leverage. I wouldn't have noticed without that hungry bird. The tree seems to call my name. Remembering that there are long nylon ropes in our packs, Jabber tries to toss one up and over the tree arm. After a few attempts, total failure—too light—need some weight for momentum.

"Got an idea, Steven; just don't shit your pants. Hang in, buddy," he says, but with little confidence in his voice.

Searching through the rucksack for something to attach to the rope for momentum, he finds the flashlight.

Taking the cord and wrapping it around the handle in a figure-eight knot, Jabs gives a mighty heave like Rocky Colavito throwing out a runner from right field: '*Runner is out at the plate—what a throw from the Rock to secure the win for the Tribe*,' as only Jimmy Dudley, voice of the Indians, could have called the action. Fans are going crazy as the flashlight-weighted cord soars up, up, and way over the limb and back into his outstretched arm.

Jabber tosses the other end of the rope for me to hold and pulls down from the tree with all his strength. Nothing. Not moving. He tries again. I'm not budging—no sucking sounds—at all.

Remembering mechanical advantage equations in physics class, I tell Jabber to take the pole, tie the rope to one end, and use the tree trunk for leverage with the other. It's like lifting up a car with a jack. Will it work?

Thanks to Sister Shelley, my horrified body begins giving off disgusting sucking sounds as Jabber, in all his, glory very slowly hoists me to safety. Can't wait to call and thank her for the memories—and for saving my life.

After recovering from the mud-sucking horror, we are still getting shot at by the crazy snipers having a ball at our expense. Like Hell Week in the ZBT house at Ohio State, 'it never ends.' Ranger live-fire drills can be anything. Obviously, low-crawl maneuvers are extremely difficult and more dangerous. An extraneous bob of the head could be career-ending for sure. The Ranger sharpshooters are probably laughing their asses off saying, "Let's see how close we can get without popping a skull or two."

Jabber chuckles, "Haha, you'll find out soon enough if you hear someone scream. You'll know if there's a misfire or accident."

The audio/video extravaganza is Disney-like—then it's not. The flood lights ignite like the bright midday sun. Sirens blare. They're stopping the exercise. Something happened.

"Emergency! Emergency! Stay where you are." Loudspeakers boom.

What the fuck—did someone get shot or bitten? Holy shit. Is this real or are they just trying to scare us? The area is vast and widespread. Nobody is very close to anyone else. In the distance we hear the unmistakable whirring of a copter and then see the red lights. A medivac. It's landing on the other side. Silence, except for creatures. Then it takes off with some poor fucker whose fate is unknown.

Loudspeakers reignite with "The exercise will continue in five minutes." The message is repeated twice as the flood lights are extinguished; the shooting begins all over again. Just like that—here one day, gone the next. I guess we'll find out later... or maybe not. The Army can be very secretive.

I like this better than the water submersion, as long it's not me they are hauling away. At least I can breathe. Can't stand up, though. Gotta crawl through the gunk over to the trees about a hundred yards away—side by side with the gators and other terrifying beasts. The place is like a sanctuary if you're on a normal tourist excursion. The magnificent vegetation offers a delightful refuge for observing critters close up and personal. Naturalists and adventurers alike seek this shit out for kicks. Personally, I hate snakes. They are disgusting, slimy, and very frightening. Don't wanna see 'em. Don't wanna touch 'em, and I really don't want to get bit by one of these fuckers. Poisonous or otherwise. The mosquitoes and no-see-'ems are ferocious—God knows what diseases they carry. Before training began, we were inoculated for every exotic and horrible illness like malaria, spotted fever, typhoid, and cholera.

"God damnit Stevie, you're going to be a platoon leader, motherfucker."

"Yeah Jabs, ...just don't want to be eaten by one of those primal monsters looking at me."

Alligators are another story. Nobody wants to mess with 'em, and they know it. Very cool. Just don't invade their territory; that's when they get cranky. There's an exceptionally large gator—has to be at least 12 feet long—his eyes focused on Jabs; his whole body heading our way.

"Those rounds get any lower, we're gonna be his lunch. It's mating season for these gators. Maybe he wants to procreate with my red hair. Only thing they like to do is fuck and eat," Jabs declares.

"So what's wrong with that?" I ask.

"Ya got me there, sucker," he replies, laughing.

Finally, getting to the nitty-gritty. Bullets, snakes, and extreme conditions threaten me. Serious shit. Lucky, or unlucky, to be chosen in the high-risk tier, better known as "SERE-C level," could be a life-altering event. This is geared to those "special" Special Forces who will experience extremely perilous operations and be placed in vulnerable situations. Exactly what I've wanted, *strived for* all my life. Be careful of what you wish for. Right, Mom?

Chapter 5

GRADUATION

Showtime: adrenaline flows from every orifice. Next time will be freaking-all-in when smelly assholes are trying to kill you or worse. It's a combination of the many preceding trials and tribulations. Graduation day from Ranger School generates real lifetime achievement awards, an astounding accomplishment. Can't believe it... a dream come true.

Our training class, formerly a group of unknown individuals from every walk of life, has completed an unimaginable Hell Week. Now, we are one—a band of brothers representing everybody who came before us, some giving their lives so that those not yet born will thrive in freedom.

SERE has been well documented: *Survival, Evasion,*

Resistance, and Escape—the mantra of Special Forces training has penetrated our psyche, branded our soul. Notwithstanding that, it sucks. It raises the limits, physically and mentally, much more intensely than the previous Ranger training tiers. Everything is geared to mastering, living, breathing, and sometimes dying for the basic premise of the Army Code of Conduct.

There are six sections, but the last component exemplifies the essence of our existence—the reason why we train until every cell in our body becomes ingrained with the Ranger sacred hymn: *Rangers Lead the Way.*

That sixth section reads 'I will never forget that I am an American, fighting for freedom, responsible for my actions, and dedicated to the principles which made my country free. I will trust in God and in the United States of America.'

This powerfully rigorous regimen requires skills that every candidate possesses, but the culmination of the extreme effort delineates those who are destined to essentially lead the masses that follow. There is a distinct difference. Everyone has a purpose on Earth, but only a select few can be cutting-edge and truly make a determination in the survival of our existence. Historically, many outlaws and contrary dissidents have tried to alter our way of life, but thankfully no one has succeeded.

Number one of The Army Ranger Code of Conduct best portrays this central core belief, the gold standard: *I am an American, fighting in the forces which guard my country and our way of life. I am prepared to give my life in their defense.*

United States military traditions are awesome. Despite the political bullshit that has been going on since the days of George Washington, all the U.S. Armed Forces graduations and moving-up days are spectacular. From West Point to Annapolis, from the U.S. Air Force Academy to the Coast Guard Academy—it's all about tradition to honor the great men and women who fight to protect our country.

Graduation day for the U.S. Army Ranger School is no exception. It begins, of course, with the National Anthem, followed by various congratulatory speeches, and ends with the famous Reviewing Party ritual which brings chills to everyone there. We all shout out the Ranger Code of Conduct in unison. It's an unbelievable experience. Afterwards we hug, reminisce, and bid farewell to the people who have come to mean so much to us. We'll all be going in our own direction; who knows when we'll see each other again?

Chapter 6

DEPLOYMENT

The weight room provides the perfect place to pass some time while the orders are processed. A few guys hop on the treadmills with their earphones blasting their brain cells, awaiting their fate. Others pump iron, building adrenaline to offset anxiety. Me... I'm just reminiscing about my BAT fraternity mischief and trying to remember the name of the girl at Geneva-on-the-Lake who gave me a great hand job during our annual summer cottage retreat.

Abundant rumors are flying that some high value targets are in our crosshairs. Maybe I can cut my teeth with these savages. Ready for the real deal, right? The directives are coming in. Our immediate future or maybe our final story. As a Ranger, you always want action; front-line stuff to corroborate and justify your training. Attention bad guys, we're coming to get you!

Breathless with anticipation, we wait for our orders. Finally, to be deployed. Man, this is it; everything I worked for, trained for, will be brought to fruition on a charming hillside in—France? Paris fucking

France!? What? Are you kidding me? Can't be accurate. Bullshit. Maybe it's a mistake. Saddam is dead, but other crazy terrorists are waiting for me. Why the fuck am I going to Paris? I can travel there on a vacation anytime. How could this happen?

Our instructions are to connect with, control, and evacuate an important Russian defector. Jabber and I are paired up as a team—and the crazy thing? He volunteered us for this mission.

"Hey Stevie, I was able to finagle the CO to match us up for this operation. Supposed to be a good one. Aren't you excited?" he asks me.

"Nothing personal, Jabs, but this mission sucks. After all that fucking training, we're going to be minding some piece-of-shit defector. That's not what I signed up for; would rather kill terrorists or blow up shit with all that fancy demolition stuff we learned about: HMX and C4 plastics. Instead, we're just going to wipe some sniveling wimp's ass. Why the fuck did you request this? What is wrong with you?" I shout.

"Thought it would be cool to be in France together. Sorry." He answers meekly.

Why would they send two brand-new Army Rangers to Paris, France for their first mission? Damn. Looks like I'm stuck with him—hard to believe this shit.

Chapter 7

I love Paris.
— Cole Porter

We fly to Rammstein Air Force Base, Germany; travel to Paris by train; and then to a safe house in the northern suburbs to await Intel updates.

On the way, Jabber and I are able to see glimpses of glorious Paris with its magnificent boulevards and the Eiffel Tower standing in the background. We cross the Seine and notice lovers everywhere holding hands, enjoying a morning walk in this heavenly city. Unfortunately, this is not a pleasure trip; strictly business. Sure enough, our coded devices, or gizmos as I like to call them, start vibrating hysterically with new instructions:

"Negate previous orders. Target is mobile. Proceed to Saint-Gaudens. Await further directives. Special handler contracted to facilitate defection. Contact information will be forthcoming."

"Roger that," I respond. "Holy shit, Jabber. The asshole was moved. Looks like we'll be going on the road again, this time straight to the mountains."

Additional information comes in. The bottom line—there is huge cash involved. The handler, known as a money-hungry piece of shit, is a facilitator of other events. Never double-crossed us before, but there's always a first time. A better deal is always lurking, and we need to extract our guy before somebody changes their mind. Understandably, the defector is scared shitless and beginning to have second thoughts. This individual is rated *extremely high value*.

We are told there are several problems associated with the defector and our operation:

1) He may or may not be a willing participant in his own removal.

2) There is a very good chance that he has been exposed and may be under extreme duress.

3) We are not the only folks looking for him. The real bad guy is Garf Zeman. He's chief of operations for the biggest state sponsor of terrorism in the world—Iran. This dude is the most dangerous motherfucker on Earth. His boss is none other than Mucza Hassan Nasrallah, head of Hezbollah. Nasrallah took over after Israel assassinated Abbas Al Musawi in 1992. Garf is his henchman and leader of the terrorist division. Brilliant and brutal—a bad combination.

4) Lastly, the French government scorns any American operations transpiring on their soil. The last U.S. bases were removed from France years ago. All their contiguous countries—including Spain, Belgium, and Italy—nurture

American troops and the endless dollar endowments that come with them, but the cigarette-smoking socialists of France look down at warmongering capitalists. Oui? Well, sometimes.

Despite these risks, the information's been deemed extremely critical with high accuracy and warrants this black-ops maneuver.

At this time, we have no other information on how to acquire a scared-to-death, motherfucking Russian. We are on a need-to-know basis. Why do I have the feeling that this isn't going to be routine?

First time is always the best: first kiss, first home run, and your first blowjob. Au revoir, Paris.

Chapter 8

Casually, we make our way to the Gare de Lyon, but have a few hours to kill. Meandering along the magnificent Champs Elysées, we stop at a great sports shop to buy supplies for the mountains. Afterward, as I promised Jabs, we grab a coffee and croissant at one of those little quaint cafés and enjoy the view and the delicious brew. The scene is electric with people promenading up and down the famous boulevard laughing and chatting with their friends. Restaurants are beginning to set up for lunch under their alluring red awnings, with staff prepping for the mad midday rush.

Paris is for lovers. Gorgeous women are everywhere—their short skirts blowing in the wind and skimpy halter tops revealing their irresistible braless boobs. Even the guys are good looking. Everyone is smiling, especially Jabber. His eyes are wide open and a big, shit-eating grin is on his face.

"Not so bad, eh Jabs?"

"Hit a home run, bro," he agrees.

"Calm down, man. Mission hasn't even started," I say.

"Yeah, it has; girls don't have underwear. Fuckin' A."

"Ha. Don't shave their armpits, either," I note.

"Party's over, man; got a train to catch," Jabs said, looking at his watch.

We could've spent the whole day there gawking at the delicious scenery, but it's time for another adventure. We catch a taxi and head to the Gare de Lyon Train Terminal, almost as glorious and recognizable as the Eiffel Tower—pure Paris.

It was built for the 1900 Paris Exposition Universelle. The magnificent clock embedded in a stately tower can be seen blocks away. It has four sides adorned with hand-painted bronze Roman numerals, like Big Ben in London. The ornate tower embracing the clock is capped with a pointed copper pergola, leaping into the sky for everyone to see the time. It has beckoned travelers for over a hundred years. Work of art, for sure. There are treasures everywhere in Paris. The city is like a museum. Can't believe the details; they couldn't build this today.

"Don't have shit like this in Michigan or Georgia, that's for sure," Jabber says. "Going to have to bring my mama here someday. C'mon Steven, let's get our asses moving and head to the hills. Gotta find this guy."

From there, we board a train to the highlands of southeast France to climb, hike, and—hopefully—secure the defector. The gear we purchased in Paris with unlimited cold hard cash from Uncle Sam is all high-end stuff: Mammut ropes, REI grappling hooks, Black Diamond climbing gloves, La Sportiva boots, GearLab belay devices,

Petzl carabiners, pitons, and some Vaughan hammers. Of course, we also bought two ultra-lightweight Western Mountaineer sleeping bags and loaded up on water and nutrition bars. Just what you'd expect from the many international climbing enthusiasts descending on the area.

We're a great team, and I trust Jabber with my life—although our pairing is not what I expected. The dynamic duo: two American tourists on their way to the mountains for a glorious vacation, rather inconspicuous. We take the Toulouse late-night train and upgrade to a modern sleeper car with a semi-private seating arrangement. Our car mates just happen to be two tantalizing young chicks who keep smiling at us—one blonde, the other brunette, heading out on their own adventure.

Jabber whispers to me, "Do you think they're interested?"

"Of course they are. We're cool," I state with authority.

"Exactly—let's go for it," he says.

"Relax, man," I tell him. "Go to sleep. You're like a wild animal just out of his cage."

"You're always right, Stevie," he says. "...need to control myself better."

"That blonde with the short skirt definitely has her eye on you, Jabber."

"Well, she's just gonna have to wait. We're on a mission Steven, remember?"

Arrive—Toulouse—07:00, but don't have time to see the sights. As a big city near the Spanish border, it's a very high-tech area and the center of the European aerospace industry. We rent a jeep, paying cash again, and make our way to Saint-Gaudens in the foothills of the Ariège Pyrenees, a grandiose area with peaks higher than 11,000 feet. The ride only takes two hours, although we stop several times to mark potential escape routes and, of course, to piss. Our route has many small turn-offs that are not noted on our map or on GPS. Navigating any one of them blindly could be hazardous and should be done only in an emergency. In the winter, they would be fun to cross-country ski.

Arriving—Saint-Gaudens—09:00, we park the Jeep in the delightful and very French city center square to check out our surroundings and wait for the shops to open. It's a popular prep area for hikers and sporting enthusiasts of all levels embarking on their own adventures.

Scanning the heights with my Steiner 15x80 binocular/rangefinder, I view the rocky overhangs, cliffs, and sheer drop-offs that are visible below the clouds. Great place to hide, if you like heights. It's becoming apparent why all the rope climbing drills are so important.

Exploring the adjacent blocks, we come upon a very cool bicycle store and purchase some awesome mountain bikes: bright yellow Yeti ARC XX1 Eagles. Remembering at the last minute, we also buy two sets of very stylish, lightweight, waterproof Gorsuch outerwear with matching pants and jackets that will come in handy in the misty upper elevations. They have pockets everywhere and hooks to attach ropes, carabiners, harnesses, or anything you would want. Mine is blue; Jabs wanted red to match his hair.

The jetsetters will be extremely jealous of our outfits, only the best for Army Rangers. Paying with cash again, we await further directives while grabbing a quick croissant and some espressos at one of the small, inconspicuous cafes.

Jabs has also insisted that we purchase exotic Prana climbing jerseys to be as stylish as possible and to attract any glamorous young ladies who happen to be nearby. He lives and preaches the old Gillette commercial, "Look sharp, be sharp." We might not know what we are doing, but we sure look good. Two wild and crazy guys off on an adventure of a lifetime.

Our dude's hidden hollow is not going to be found on a tourist map in this extremely rugged area with sky-high plateaus and rockslide remnants in every direction. Once off the main paths, travel will be treacherous.

According to the latest update, the handler is to move our target to a remote expanse in the Ariège region of the Pyrenees Mountains, the exact location unknown at this time. It is surmised that the final handoff will be in one of the hundreds of mystical caves. The area is famous for its prehistoric grottoes, many of which have remarkable artwork—a living museum.

The Pyrenees Mountains are a natural boundary between France and Spain. The breathtaking but rugged landscape has been used and abused by many armies over the millennia for secure refuge and surprise onslaughts from positions of advantage and camouflage. Adversarial incursions have taken place for thousands of years as legions of doom plotted assaults from sanctuaries within steps of our locale. The highest plateaus are above the tree line and provide ideal observatories.

Recalling geology class, the Pyrenees were formed around sixty million years ago from a collision between the Iberian and the much larger Eurasian landmass. Additionally, the glacial retraction further delineated the extreme rock formation and provided an incredibly unique safe haven, as well as strategic bases for counter-resurgence. Few environments on Earth nurture this type of inner sanctum.

These harsh mountains are integrated with profoundly picturesque portals of exit providing natural drainage and run off. As geological plates retreated from their origin, gutters of water propulsion generated vast chasms of tributaries providing Mother Earth a mechanism to nurture and sustain her geological descendants. As glacial retraction accelerated, subterranean rivers drilled hydro-offshoots extending through millennial rock formations and evolved as cavernous existential sewers commonly known as caves.

Notwithstanding, the genesis of many mountain ranges, except for volcanoes, were generally birthed through water expulsion mechanisms. Natural catharsis propelled hydro-generated escape hatches like giant farts.

Additional coded messages come in as our devices snort,

"Proceed to Lorp-Sentaraille in the Pyrenees... blah, blah, blah. Await further directives."

"Roger that," I answer. "We're headed to the caves, Jabber; our canary awaits us."

Chapter 9

Surrounded by stately cypress trees growing out of thick underbrush, we drive on unmarked paths for an hour with the bikes strapped to the back of the car. Purposely using old trails, we never come across any other adventurers. They have the common sense to remain in the well-traveled areas.

Rapidly approaching Lorp-Sentaraille, a small commune with about fifteen hundred people, we begin to scout out a remote area where we can hide the car. It's our final jumping off point before the trek up. According to the intelligence, this commune is very private; everybody keeps to themselves. There are just a few restaurants and hotels—not much to do. That's the attraction.

We come upon a heavily camouflaged path with very dense scrub-grass and a grouping of some beech and fir trees to the side that offers great refuge for the Jeep until later. We off-load the Yetis and rucksacks, then continue, not knowing what might lie ahead. It will be an adventure, for sure. The rest of the mission will be a combination of biking, trekking, and mountain climbing. Sounds great but, somehow, I have a strange feeling that it's not going to be a pleasure trip. Things are way too easy.

"Just the two of us, my friend. They must think we're great partners," says Jabber.

"You bet, never done shit like this before, Jabs. Just a rookie out of Ohio State."

Walking the bikes for a while to gain our bearings and check the area, we hike through a captivating meadow filled with poppies, the juxtaposition of ruggedness and splendor only God, the artist, could have created.

Jabber seems uncharacteristically quiet. Not sure what's wrong.

"You okay, Jabs?"

"Perfect, just miss those honeys from the train. Feel we could've had something going," he laments.

"Time for that stuff later," I say.

Meanwhile, I'm getting some sort of monkey business on my device. It keeps pinging, almost like it's got malware or something, except this device has an extra feature—when an unauthorized party tries to hop on our signal, it starts to ping. We are obviously being monitored, but by whom? Real strange shit's happening; not sure what.

"Jabber, we're being isolated," I warn him. "I don't like things that can't be explained."

"You, my friend, are a paranoid motherfucker," he scoffs.

"...think you're in denial," I reply.

"Stevie, I have to piss," he says. "...will be right back. Going behind those trees," he says, pointing to the woods about fifty feet away.

While he's taking a leak, I examine my gizmo to make sure everything is working. Checking that pinging, I hear Jabs unintelligibly mumbling about something, and then a pause, then mumbling again. After a few minutes, he comes scampering back and says he's ready to rock.

"Ok, let's go. By the way, who were you talking to?" I ask.

"Oh, just myself; helps me piss better. I'm my best listener, ya know," he replies, laughing.

I check my pack to be cautious and make sure my knife is with me. You never can tell when you're going to need it. Phew, there it is. Love this bad boy, my Benchmade Griptilian, almost as much as the Swiss Army knife from the Cleveland Heights Cub Scouts. Lots of guys like the Leatherman all-purpose tool; some carry both—not me. Bench, all the way.

Only a few people, not including Jabber or me, know the exact whereabouts of our asset. We'll find out soon enough. The Ariège region is remote, and the cavern is not on any map.

There is no need to go into the town and risk exposure; the mission is dangerous enough. A small, abandoned route appears up ahead and offers a secluded spot to begin our ascent to the lower escarpment.

The mountain bikes are perfect for this section. They'll have to be discarded when we move to the extreme verticals. Actually, I'm looking forward to that part... remembering the horror of the first few parachute jumps until I felt exhilaration through confidence. *Ahhh.*

Maybe I am paranoid. Sure, we know that ops are observing us for our protection, but with all that pinging, there are clearly other folks out there. The intelligence world is everywhere.

We bike up the path, stopping every few minutes to catch our breath. It's tough going and our legs start to burn, but we're making steady progress. The real hard part is yet to come—rock climbing— won't be easy, but I'm ready for the challenge.

Up ahead, there's a plateau where we can stop and review some new data about the defector while we reevaluate our next step. Intelligence updates are pouring in. Everything is in real time; our devices are rocking.

Finally reaching the small mesa, we hop off the bikes, drink plenty of water, and enjoy the spectacular view of the Ariège plain. We are now 2000 feet above Lorp-Sentaraille, which looks like a dot on a map. Intelligence is giving us the thumbs up to continue. We are closing in, but they want us to move laterally for a while.

To succeed, the facilitator will have to make himself available to our intelligence ops so they can pinpoint the rendezvous. The caves in the area are enormous. Some of them meander miles with hundreds of tributaries and pathways. If someone doesn't want to be found, they could hide here forever. Our support team back home or wherever really needs to get us close enough to establish communication before anyone else finds him—especially motherfucking Garf Zeman. It's a race against time.

We break down the incredibly light carbon-fiber bikes by removing the front wheels and latching them to the main frames. This allows us to connect them to our Arc'teryx harnesses along with the backpacks and lug them up the mountain—great training exercise for football.

With the Yetis hooked to our backs, we begin a series of rappelling maneuvers to get closer to the other side of the peak. Hopefully, by that time, our people will enlighten us with the defector's whereabouts. That is just the beginning. We'll have to secure the asset and then evacuate him from this Godforsaken, breathtaking part of the world.

After moving left for a while in hopes of reaching the trail, we need to get to the rocky shelf just around the next curvature. To do this, we must swing ourselves to build momentum and land on the ledge about ten yards away. We anchor a grappling mechanism to a huge boulder, leaving enough slack on each rope to allow ourselves a complete full arc swing to the shelf across the way. The length and slack must be perfect or it won't work, and the consequences will be fatal. Fuck, this is not going to be easy.

"Watch out for those stones; they're coming right down on us. Duck your head in so they can bounce off the helmet," I warn Jabber.

Suddenly, he starts singing the great song "Nowhere to Run."

"Martha and the Vandellas, written by Eddie Holland," I

inform him.

"Good memory. Just don't look down, Stevie boy," he warns.

Ok, ok, gonna do this. Did it before, piece of cake. No problem. There's a small shelf just around the curve and a trail extension beyond. Got to get around this bend and... and...

Jabs swings first. Just like kids playing with a rope tied to a big tree branch. Up and down. Higher and higher and then—down. Then up, up, and away. Perfect two-point landing, like in the Olympics. Boom. The crowd is going nuts. Score: 9.9!

"No problem, Stevie. I'll make my way over there and guide you in. There's plenty of rope, and we're protected by our sling. Attached at the hip forever, you and me, babe," he yells over a loud rumbling noise.

Rocks start falling everywhere. Landslide. Rockslide. Can't even see him. Dust envelopes the whole area—looks like fog. Zero visibility. Just like the great Carole King song, "I Feel the Earth Move." Should have paid more attention to the geology professor, always thought those mandatory classes were a waste of time. Look at us now.

"Jabs, you alright? Where are you, man? Can't see you!"

"Fuck, can't get a grip with my boots," Jabber shouts. "Starting to slip, shit. Slipping. Help me, Steven! Help!"

Can hear but can't see him... only twenty feet away; could have been a mile. All I sense is the thumping and reverberation of rocks falling and exploding into dust. It's unbelievable—out of a bright blue day comes chaos generated by nature. Jabs is in the wrong place at the wrong time.

Have to do something to save him. He is helpless and getting battered by the rock storm.

"Hey Jabs, can you hear me? You ok? Don't worry, we're connected!" I scream. "Coming to get you. Hang on, bro."

He's been pummeled off the plateau and is swaying like a pendulum. "Fuck, should never have gone to Michigan," he says.

"All forgiven; just hang tight," I encourage him.

"That's the problem. Hanging. Gonna die!" he moans.

"No, you're not," I command, shimming over there. "Try not to sway so much."

"Ha, fuck you!" he yells. "Easy for you to say."

"Coming," trying to calm him down. "Ok, now I can see what's going on."

His rope is still connected to the grappling hook and to my sling, but all hell is breaking loose. Rocks are flying everywhere. Jabs is getting bashed. Have to help him, my new bud. He's hanging midway between the two ledges, just swaying.

The rock storm is letting up, so this is my last chance to get to him before he loses consciousness. Looks like he was in a gang war. Can't believe it didn't kill him. There is blood dripping everywhere—from his scalp and face, pure horror. The helmet is gone.

Without really thinking, I swing over to him and grab on for dear life. Looking dazed, he smiles and kisses my forehead, just like my mom.

"Hi, Stevie," he says with blood coming out of his nose and mouth.

"Hi James, must get you over to the other side."

"How ya gonna do that?" he asks pessimistically.

"Push you man, gonna push you over there. Just pretend you're on a swing in the park," I say, "like when you were a kid. Ok?"

"Yeah, boss. Let's do it," he answers without hesitation.

Letting go, we're hanging by our individual ropes. I try to push and swing him over to the other plateau, but he's like dead weight and can't build momentum.

The only option is to elevate together as one unit and then drop him on the ledge. Interlocking my left arm with his harness, I begin to slowly swing. First, just a few feet back and forth. Then, a little higher and a little farther, like on the playground. I'm exhausted, but we are almost to the ledge. Just a little more, one more swing. Back, back, and then, with all my strength, using my right arm to push off the rock face, Jabs and I become one person. We are soaring like a giant trapeze. For one brief moment in time, we are in the circus.

Reaching the pinnacle of momentum, I let go and fling him to other side. He makes it. Goddamn son-of-a-bitch. He's smashed up like a bloody pulp but, astonishingly, there he is waving and giving me instructions. I'm now suspended by my own rope. He's on the other ledge egging me on. Despite his bloodied face and certain discomfort, Jabber is coaching me.

"It's nice here, Stevie. Great view. C'mon over. Start swinging like you did with me."

I freeze. A few seconds ago with Jabs, I never had time to think; just did it. Now, I can't move—just hanging in the breeze.

"Swing, swing, and then jump. Just do it!" Jabs yells.

Hanging like a sack of shit, I remember the terror of my first parachute jump:

Suddenly, the jump zone alert blares with flashing yellow lights and a probing foghorn sequence, 'On deck. On deck. On deck.'

Oh fuck.

Harsh penetrating lights violate my eyes. Deafening sounds reverberate through my eardrums. Spasms of pain rock my body. Head exploding. Hyperventilating. Nauseous. Time stands still. All sounds become one; don't understand. Flashing lights everywhere. I'm paralyzed.

"Jump, you fucking asshole, or I'll shoot!" the CO screams.

Back to reality—time stands still. I see myself in a different perspective, like a super-athlete who can visualize everything in slow motion. Great hitters can see the seams spin on a baseball. Wide receivers catch a football and precisely tiptoe along the sideline like a ballerina.

I jump.

"YAY!" Jabs cheers as he watches me make a perfect landing. "Unbelievable! You're going to win the gold medal." He hugs me. "Son of a bitch. You saved my life, Steven. Goddamn!"

"Did it together, Jabs. Awesome team," smiling back. "You don't look so good. Got to dress your wounds."

"Screw that. I'm ok," he says, "just a few bumps and bruises. I'll wash off the blood and be good as new. Just need to rest for a few minutes."

"Me too," sighing a big sigh.

The next leg is going back up again, but this time we are on the other side of the curvature. This is a triathlon for the ages; going to be tired tonight—could sure use a cold 'Black Label' beer. That gets me thinking back to my high school days when I was trying to stockpile beer for our summer cottage.

Chapter 10

GENEVA-ON-THE-LAKE

As the end of June 1963 approached, the anticipation of the summer climax at the cottage began to increase. Everything was going as planned. The acquisition of food was about halfway complete. There were approximately six weeks before the big blowout. That would certainly be enough time to accumulate and stockpile enough nourishment to sustain us for two weeks on the shores of Lake Erie. Six weeks meant at least that many fancy open house parties that would allow the benevolent BATs to honor their hosts with housewarming gifts. Our concept of housewarming was different than most. The bounty marched out the door. It was for a good cause.

The stockpiling of beer, on the other hand, was not proceeding well. In fact, it seemed to diminish as time went on. The good brothers were depleting the inventory faster than we were able to replenish it. If this were a large company, a second and third shift protocol would have to be implemented. According to the laws of economics, either we acquired more product or decreased the daily consumption to build up an adequate reserve for the future. We needed to accumulate two weeks of brew inventory to satisfy the insatiable thirst of the BATs and any invited guests, namely females.

So, let's do the math. Six weeks to go and our supply was being consumed at the rate of sixteen cases per day. At that burn rate and current acquisition pace of new product, we would run out of beer one week before the festivities at Geneva-on-the-Lake commenced. Therefore, an emergency intervention was required to triple our stock over the next six weeks just to make sure.

There was only one solution: call in the troops. We enlisted older brothers and sisters, neighbors, or anyone with real or fake ids. Whatever it took. We worked day and night and started to make headway, but we fell short. With just one week to go, we hit the break-even point. That is, input and output stabilized but we were not able to accumulate any excess. We were so close and yet so far away. It was out of the question to inaugurate our cottage sabbatical with an inadequate supply of suds. We were BATs. We would not falter.

As president and operations leader, it was up to me. Suddenly, at 4 a.m., when the best ideas came my way, I received a revelation. Mabel and I almost had a wet dream. For those of you who remember, Mabel was that famous raunchy barmaid in the television commercial, "Hey Mabel, Black Label." Earlier that spring, I had noticed a Help Wanted ad for the Carling Brewery Company targeted to college students. Like most large wineries and breweries, they promoted their products with samples and tasting sessions. Why hadn't I thought of this earlier?

The next day, I summoned the brothers for an emergency meeting and told them of my plan. All the guys who had fake IDs were instructed to apply for jobs at Carling, down in the 'flats' along the infamous and very flammable Cuyahoga River. The brewery was constructed in the last century and looked its age. It was a dark and foreboding warehouse with huge copper vats that were connected with elongated corroded steam-emitting pipes that appeared like the monsters from the horror movie 'Them.' Rumors were rampant that their water supply came from the river. As the cases of beer came off the assembly line, our job would be to stack them on wooden skids. That seemed easy enough until we did it for 15 minutes. Six cases of beer in each row stacked five high—it was hard to do for five minutes, very difficult for an hour, and practically impossible for a full day. As I looked around, everyone else had made a career of skid loading. Wow. Two guys paired up for each skid. They worked in unison... perfect harmony. The fourth and fifth rows were the most exhausting because the cases had to be lifted the highest. Once loaded, the wooden beast was replaced within fifteen seconds by an empty monster. You had about 60 seconds to rest your burning muscles before the torture repeated.

Our foreman was this enormous black dude, Leroy, a great guy. He had gone to Cleveland Glenville High School and had played linebacker at a junior college before having a tryout with the Browns. He made their taxi squad for a year before being cut. Now he was married with two little girls and had a very limited future. He was foreman of this particular assembly line, but probably had advanced as far as he could. This certainly was a lesson in life. Being the manager of conveyor belt #17 at the Carling Brewery was not on my top ten list of goals.

Leroy was cool. He understood that we would only be there for a few weeks and that our rather short-term goal was to obtain as much beer as we could. We soon realized that he was going to be our savior. With Leroy's help, it was a piece of cake to load an endless amount of beer into our cars at the conclusion of each shift. We invited him as our VIP guest to the BAT summer extravaganza. Leroy was very excited. Not only had he made friends with kids from the suburbs, he had also temporarily extended his horizon past football and the slums. So, with one day to spare, we officially reached our beer goal thanks to our new best friend. Our brewski problems were solved and Leroy was about to spend the best two weeks of his life as an honorary BAT.

Chapter 11

If I ever get back to Cleveland, the first thing I'm gonna do is grab an ice cold Black Label and kiss Mabel. But I'm a long way off; I've gotta focus on the here and now. I notice Jabber checking out the climbing gear, then rechecking to make sure the harnesses fit snugly. Recharged after some disgusting MREs and lots of water, we are on to the next terrifying leg of our assignment. First, I manage to climb through a series of lateral switchbacks to reach a flat ledge a hundred feet higher than where I began. Takes me over an hour, but now I can secure a rope around a big boulder so we can haul the bikes up. Jabber follows, climbing the rope straight up. There are a lot of loose rocks everywhere, but this time—no blood.

"Hey Jabs, we were able to do this over 12-foot swells from that Apache. Only shit my pants once and that was after puking all over my Army boots," I remind him.

"Didn't want to tell you Stephen, but I puked too," he admits.

"Really? Fuckin' A. Well, get ready for more barfing. Going to be climbing up, down, and sideways," I inform him.

"Haha, this is the real deal, man. Just you and me," he responds.

"Wouldn't want it any other way, Jabs," I assure him. "Rock on, buddy, and that's not a pun."

Jabber pukes once on his ascent but now here he is. His grin and his red flaming hair emerge over the lip of the ledge, and he's asking me, "What's for lunch?"

After sitting there for a few minutes and collecting ourselves, we make our way down the tiny path which soon broadens and merges with an old stone road. After surveying the surroundings and checking out our GPS location, we realize we're too open and vulnerable.

"Don't like it," I say. "Need to get moving."

Soon, we notice an old lift ahead, most likely the gondola referenced on the map. Oh, man. Not happy about how it looks.

"Don't know if I can do this, Jabs. Fuck."

"Just do it," he says, "like the helo dunker. You're a pro, Stevie. I'll get you through it. Remember you told me, 'We're a team.'"

"That's right. Fuckin' dynamic duo," I say, smiling.

We have to find the facilitator and the defector. The gondola looks like the best way to get to the southern-facing peak with all those enchanting caves. The geography and topography are uncharted, as is this whole affair.

"Jabber. Don't know man. Look at this fucking piece of shit," I moan.

According to our intel, the gondola is a German remnant of the forties. Nasty looking, it's a rusted-out hunk of junk, suspended by a single corroded steel cable, twelve thousand feet over the rocks below. Shit. How are we gonna get out? Gonna snap. Today's gonna be the day. Watch, just my luck. Worse than the helo, only one window. Oh, man. Serotonin receptors kick in, nothing to give 'em except nauseating anxiety.

"Ughhh," I groan.

Seeing that I'm a little tentative, Jabber says, "Stevie, make you some frog soup if you get out alive, haha." Jabber keeps shaking his head and smirking. "Got your ass covered; ya know I wouldn't let anything happen to you."

"What the hell are you talking about? No frogs here," I point out.

"Betcha there are," he says. "For sure there are snakes; maybe I can cook you up some big juicy rats with some crawfish étouffée. Then we can watch some football."

"Do you even know what's coming out of your mouth?" I ask.

"To tell you the truth," he says, "sometimes I don't. Better than puking."

This tin can is like an old elevator in downtown Cleveland that failed its last inspection. Shit.

But I follow my wacky red-headed partner inside. When he turns the power on from the inside switch, the door closes automatically. For safety reasons, our intel tells us, it will only open when we reach the exit ledge—if we ever make it. Feel like a mummy in a tomb with no way out. Fuck me. Panic is overwhelming my body.

Getting that fucking helo-dunker feeling—I remember it vividly. Whoa! Can feel that fear. Claustrophobic. Take some deep breaths and envision myself in the surf on a South Carolina barrier island.

"Ughhh," I groan.

Can't get out if I wanted to. When the gondola arrives at the landing platform, the door will open automatically, *if* you believe in fairy tales. At least I brought my WD-40... just in case... ya never know. Comes in handy when you least expect it—always part of my rucksack. Looking at this rat trap, we just may need it in case the latch won't open.

"Gonna puke all over your new boots and your ugly red hair. If you get me out, we'll go find the honeys from the train," I say nauseously.

"Oh, don't get personal. Love you, man. Stevie, this is so much easier than the dunker... not under water... just lots of air. You'll be ok. Trust me," Jabs replies, trying to calm down.

It's a perfect storm for my phobias to rebel—claustrophobia vs. acrophobia. Breathing becomes almost impossible. Nightmares are not this horrible. *Breathe. Breathe.* Supposed to be a high-level Ranger with phenomenal talents and intestinal fortitude. There's nothing I can't overcome.

The contraption seems like it's moving one inch an hour. Clink. Clink. Clink. Now it's moving even slower. We're never gonna make it. Clink... clink.

"Going crazy, Jabs. Fuck! Get me the fuck out of here now, Jabber, right now," I plead.

He's not paying attention to my whining; can't blame him. Gonna die in this fucking metal tomb, just like the helo dunker. Goddamn Germans.

"Breathe. Breathe," I keep reminding myself.

"Hahaha," shrieks Howdy Doody. "Hahaha."

"Gonna kill you, Jabber, you fuckin' asshole!" I threaten.

Chapter 12

Struggling to survive the next moment, I catch a glimpse of the foreboding cliff with the platform, but the gondola is almost stationary. Approaching the landing plateau seems to take an eternity. Barely a movement.

Clink. Then nothing. It stalled—stopped fucking short of the ledge. No more clinks, but the wind offers its share of horror rocking the tin can back and forth.

My worst nightmare. God. What are we gonna do now? How do we get over there? Jesus. The cord has stretched through the years and created a dip, so jumping over is impossible. The door's six agonizing feet from the platform and 12,000 feet above mean jagged rocks below. The only solution is to shimmy the last few yards, hand over hand under the cable. But the exit must open first—please, God!

How the hell do we exit if we can't open the fucking door from the inside? "Get me out of here right now!" I scream, "before I pee in my pants!"

Pits are pitting out; balls are retracting into their homeland, and then...

A loud, bizarre clanging noise emanates from the old rusty

mechanized opener. It's working. Wow—don't even need the WD-40; I'll save it for a rainy day.

Watching in awe—the nuts, bolts, chains, and pulleys automatically begin their progressions; the door commences its opening protocol. An astounding moment. This freaking antique apparatus from the Stone Age is moving. Will it be enough?

"Hahaha. Maybe this is how it's done on the space station," Jabs laughs.

"What space station?" I ask. "What are you talking about? Like a spacewalk?"

"Yeah man," he says. "You'll be an astronaut. Just shimmy up that cable. No problem. Hahaha, only two miles up. Not like we're in orbit or something."

"You're going first, fuckface ," I demand, looking down at the distant rocks.

Our devices start to roar again, exploding with this message:

'NEED TO MAKE CONTACT WITH HANDLER ASAP. DETAILS OF LOCATION WILL FOLLOW. VERIFY.'

"Roger," I respond.

The wind conditions are getting much worse, causing a huge horizontal sway, back and forth. Getting seasick in this rusty tomb— feels like the ocean swells from the parachute exercise over water. Meanwhile, the fucking Russian defector is in some cave nearby whacking off. The handler is probably watching him sack his sausage, and our backup team is surely sucking down beer and pizza somewhere on the Champs Elysées while we're trapped here— maybe forever.

Chapter 13

I'm not afraid of death; I just don't want to be
there when it happens.
— Woody Allen

The winds are calming down a bit; this is our opportunity to perform our daredevil act—time to start shimmying.

"Maybe I'll find a gorgeous princess in a cave," Jabs rants as he leads the way through the now-opened door and very easily hoists himself up to the cable. He is so good, maybe he was in the circus definitely in the freak show.

Just to be safe, he uses a belt harness and special Dainese Kevlar gloves we purchased in Paris. In the blink of an eye, he's standing on the platform beckoning me to join him.

"C'mon out here man," he joshes. "The weather is spectacular. On my way to San Jose."

"You gotta be nuts to do what you just did. Fucking crazy!" I tell him through my own trepidation.

"Let's go, Stevie. The chicks are waiting; they want to party hard." He kids me, but I am not in a jovial mood.

"Gonna piss my pants, Jabs. Holy shit. Fuuuuuck!" … I hear myself scream, but am unable to stop.

Suddenly, when all seems lost, I develop a profoundly strange urge—hunger. Bodily functions are bizarre. At a moment in time when an anxiety attack seems imminent, I get famished, ravenously starved. Incredibly, the anatomical and physiological battles whose ugly heads always rear during these spells begin to decelerate. I can only focus on my next meal.

"Fuck. Get over here! Leaving to find my princess," he mockingly informs me.

"What's for lunch?" I ask sincerely.

"Are you crazy?" he replies.

"Seriously. Can't have any more MREs. Hate 'em. How about some Ketel One and steak?" I beg.

The Army has not changed operational rations since World War II. They just get different names: "D" rations or "K" rations, sustenance with zero pleasure. Bottom line—they are awful and earn their label, "shit on a stick."

"Well, fuck off; that's all we have," he replies arrogantly.

"Jabber, I will not exit this enchanting chariot unless you promise we will have a delicious cassoulet for lunch."

"No steak on the menu today," he reports in earnest, "just goat. Cassoulet is out of the question. It takes at least a day to prepare."

"By the way Jabs, what are we gonna do with these booyah bikes?" I ask.

"Only one thing to do," he responds. "Throw 'em over the edge. Smoosh the fuckers."

"That's a total waste of money," I say. "Oh well, the government wastes money every day. Chalk this up to a business expense. It'll be fun watching them bounce off the rocks on the way down. Ha! You'll be able to see what would happen to one of us," I point out.

"Exactly... can't wait!" he responds, giggling.

Back to the cassoulet—it's a local dish, sort of a potpie with various fresh ingredients like cabbage, meat, or seafood. Anything is acceptable if it tastes great. There are infinite variations depending on the availability of produce.

"Need a cassoulet now, Jabs," I demand.

"Sorry to break your heart, but cassoulet is unavailable as the chef has not returned from marketing. Probably died," Jabs reports with a straight face.

"Well then, let's have jambon, fromage, and some local wine. Ok?" I ask.

"Alright. Maybe some aligot, bread, and garbure," he suggests impatiently. "Let's go. C'mon Steven, get the fuck out of there."

"Trying, really. Have to prepare my body," I inform him.

"What the fuck are you talking about?"

"Need to poop. You should never eat before moving your bowels," I say, very matter-of-factly.

"Go over in the rocks and shit to your heart's content. After you've finished, we'll be trekking down to the 7K level, and we'll seek out some grub. First, get out of your chariot, now!"

"Ok, if you insist, but be nice; just remember I can kick the crap out of you, Jabs!" I inform him.

"Just take care of business," he orders me in no uncertain terms.

"Wow... remembering this adorable girl," I tell him, smiling ear to ear.

"Who, your magic princess cheerleader from high school?" he asks.

"A little delight who gave me a huge blowjob and then, and then... don't remember anymore. Whatever—mus... must... must've been a dream," I lament.

"Did you cum?" Jabs asks, with anticipation.

"My mom woke me up," I say.

"Oh man, that's a bummer," he says. "But if you want to start talking about blowjobs, I remember going to this joint with all kinds of dudes who just stuck their dicks in the wall and got an instant suck from the other side. Called glory holes. Don't really know if it was a girl, a guy, or a donkey. Could have been a monkey. I was sure mine was a ravishing girl with long blonde hair and sexy legs. She told me she loved me and wanted to get married."

Jabber just keeps talking about some girl who gave him a big juicer or something and then a whole litany of unintelligible words. The Jabs is on a roll.

"Did you ever actually see her?" I ask.

"No, they had special rules," he says. "You couldn't go to the other side of the wall, or you'd be thrown out for life. But I knew she was exquisite, and she loved me."

"How did you know?" I ask.

"Because she told me so. It was busy that night and a lot of guys were waiting in line. She told me to come back real soon, and we could plan the wedding," he says, affectionately.

"Jabs, she said that to get you to finish up quickly. You're a real lover, but man—can't you stop talking, just for a minute?" I plead.

"Whew! When I stop, I think I'm gonna croak," he answers with a big sigh.

"Well then, perhaps you should stop—ha!" I suggest.

The increasingly rugged terrain is now inaccessible for biking, so the Yeti Arc Eagles have to be discarded from the gondola before I exit. Can't get 'em to the other side anyway—too difficult—and don't want 'em left behind in case someone is tracking us. The big problem will be getting me out of here—but first things first.

Bombs away, as they say. The noise of metal smashing into the rocks sounds like a car wreck. Then, as the remnants plunge out of sight to the depths below, the pathetic sound is absorbed by the wind in the vast escarpment.

"Good job, Stevie boy—these eagles don't fly," he yells, with a little mischief in his voice. "Look how far they bounced off the side of the cliff; it's probably the tires. Wow. This is fun!"

"Holy shit, not a pretty sight. What a shame!" I moan.

Maybe it's the impending thought of a succulent lunch or the hideous vision of watching the bikes smash; my contrary body suddenly relaxes and allows me to easily scamper out to the very impatient Jabber.

"Finally, you chicken shit," he scoffs. "Go take a crap in those woods over there."

"Thank you," I reply. "It looks very comfortable behind those rocks. Constipated—it may take a while. Wow... there... yeah. Perfect spot."

I find a nice, secluded area to dump my load and suddenly—wouldn't you know it—my gizmo starts buzzing uncontrollably with a directive to use my privacy earpiece for more security. It's perplexing how these things always happen when you're least prepared to answer.

"Attention Steven, highest level security from COVAC: Jabber is compromised, repeat Jabber is compromised. Must be terminated, repeat, must be terminated at all costs. Respond 'roger' with your code to verify communication, and to authenticate receipt of transmission."

My encrypted satellite device is having an orgasm. Wow. How can this be? Jabber's my best buddy; friends since the first day of training. What a dumpster fire—ripping my guts out. Holy fuck; gotta be wrong. It'd be like killing family. Starting to puke. Can't kill him. We're best friends. He got me through training. Saved his life; he saved mine.

Thinking back, maybe it was too obvious—always him and me, side-by-side. Shoulda realized. Shit, there's no such thing as a coincidence. Very strange indeed. Can't believe I have to kill him. Just saved his life and now I must do him in. Jesus. Things don't add up. Too many missteps with Jabber.

"C'mon, finish up; no wonder you've been cranky," Jabs pleads.

"Trying—not easy in these fuckin' woods," I say as I enter my code and ask for clarification.

Seconds later, the response arrives.

"Discovered Jabs is a plant from Iran. Set up twenty years ago when parents immigrated. Jabber does not know his parents are in custody. His own mission is to kill you and the facilitator. Details will follow. Terminate ASAP. VERIFY."

Nooooo. Can't kill him. Can't. My best friend. Gonna puke. Fuck, nooooo. Why? Why me? Oh God. Nooooo.

"What is the confidence level of this info?" I ask.

"100%," is the agonizing reply from COVAC.

I'm shaking like a leaf.

What should I do? How can I kill him? ...can't believe this. Fuck, no. Oh man. Gotta take out my BFF. Holy shit! Can't use a gun... too noisy. Never killed anybody before... gotta think. Used to do homework on the toilet... helps clear my brain. Should talk to him first... two sides to every story; maybe mistaken identity. Goddamnit. Shit.

Chapter 14

Plop, plop, fizz, fizz, oh what a relief it is.
— Bayer

After relieving myself, I feel so much better. It's wonderful what a good dump will do for your brain cells. Gotta focus on Jabber now with a clean colon and a clear head.

"Man, that was a four-star poop," I tell Jabs proudly.

"So happy for you, Stevie boy. Hurry the fuck up," he orders.

"Ok, ok. Yeah, just finishing up Jabs, takes time; pooping in the woods is an art form. Much better on my own toilet. Be right over there, man," I tell him.

The transponder is a hybrid of a miniature satellite phone (with voice encryption) and a new high-tech pager/messaging device. It possesses an extremely sophisticated encoding system developed by the Israelis, and supposedly cannot be hacked—but that pinging... To think this asshole is plotting against the Rangers, America, and me is repulsive. Time to rise up, take care of business, and make my mother proud. Now that's what I call a fortuitous dump!

Chapter 15

You believe lies so you eventually learn to trust no
one but yourself.
— *Marilyn Monroe*

"Ok, feelin' much better. Thanks for being so understanding," I say with a big grin.

"No problem, Stevie. When ya gotta go, ya gotta go," he answers with an even bigger grin.

"Like a dog; can shit five times a day," I report very factually.

"Thought you were constipated." he says.

"Not anymore. Let's move out," I tell him firmly.

"Yeah, ok. Be careful! Gonna be dangerous!" he warns.

We are just above the clouds, and ice is forming everywhere from the condensation. It's very slippery. When air cools, water condenses; if the temperature is below freezing, you get ice. That's what Sister Shelley said. Should look her up some time; very cute, and she's a nun.

Man, you could get hurt on these tiny paths. Maybe I'll just throw him over the cliff. Nah. That would be too easy, and I wouldn't be able to confirm the kill. Frickin' treacherous with all this ice; could slide right off myself and land on the top of those pine trees. No one would ever find us except the eagles. This is like a bobsled track except we don't have a sled. Stay focused. Don't want to get myself killed before I whack him.

"Hey Jabs, you can always take one of those new, fancy gondolas on the western escarpment that the skiers and hikers use lots of windows," I say sarcastically.

"Not a good idea, Steven," he warns. "Someone could spot us. Gotta hoof it. Very dangerous going down these trails—but no other way. Too much exposure. We'll utilize switchbacks so we can descend without killing ourselves."

Although early July, there are still snow-entombed peaks. Trekking is very difficult until we approach the 9,000 foot-elevation snow line. Some of the caves with a southern exposure are starting to reveal themselves in the slowly emerging sunlight. We'll be going up there. Should be interesting—whole different world. People lived in those caves for thousands of years.

"Wow, famished," I start, reluctantly pulling out an MRE and devouring it like a Big Mac.

"Steve, all you ever do is eat or think about eating," he tells me.

"What's wrong with that? You left out fucking," I correct him.

"Sorry," Jabs replies. "Be careful on these paths, Steven. Really steep and icy."

"Yeah, scary looking down there. Right behind you, man," I assure him.

Have to keep a visual on him at all times. The paths become narrower as they get steeper. It's him against me, but he doesn't know I know. Ya don't know what ya don't know. Be a killing machine. Act like a man, motherfucker, even though he's my best friend. Damn, what a turn of events.

The thought of killing my partner is making me fuckin' sick. Bad enough when ya have to take out someone you don't know, but not my best friend. Fuck. Goddamnit. We trained together, went through all that shit together. Gotta find out what he knows before I do him in.

Traversing the switchbacks is treacherous enough due to the sheer drop-offs but, to make matters worse, the summer thaw is at its peak. Many of the trails that are below the freeze line are like water slides in a fun-and-games park with no safety net.

Jabber and I are flying by the seat of our pants—out of control—barely able to keep our footing when he hits an extreme vertical. I'm about fifty yards behind as he vanishes. His scream, however, tells me everything I need to know—he's gone.

"Jabber," I yell. "Where are you?"

Losing sight of him is unnerving; I fully expect to get a bullet through the back of my head. They say you never hear the shot that blows your skull apart.

There is no answer as I scramble down to his last position.

"Jabber, you motherfucker, what the fuck is going on?" I plead.

No sound, nothing; just the wind swirling between the canyon walls. Oh shit, he must know—gonna ambush me. Probably would have but he needs my help to secure the asset.

Chapter 16

This is not happening.

"Jabber!" I call out. "Say something... anything! ...need to find you so I can help..."

Suddenly I hear a moan—and then another. "Jabber, talk to me. Do something. I took first-aid courses and can save you—don't know where you are. C'mon Jabber, fart or..."

"Fuck off. Ah... ahm here. Rescue me... Focus... need your help. Forget about th'—about th' Goddamn phobias. M'life is in ya hands," he pathetically pleads.

It sure is; he doesn't know the half of it. Can't even manage my own life.

"I, I, ah, need you to help me—to help you, Jabs. C'mon, give me a sign," I say, "anything, you fucking asshole. Where are you?"

"Look down, you prick ... look down," he moans.

"Where?"... thinking he has the drop on me.

"Here, over the edge," he groans.

Finally see him about three stories below, propped up like a pig on a stick. "Oh shit, Jabs!" I gasp.

"Yep," is all he can muster.

"Howdja get down there?" I ask, incredulous. "What happened, Jabs?"

"Slipped. Frickin' ledge. Landed on mah back," he mutters. "Need your help to get outta here."

"Jabber, hold on. I'm coming. Hang in there," I encourage him.

I don't trust this fucker, not at all. He's trying to kill me. Concentrate—it's him or me. Live or die.

A dazzling canvas—Jabber lying in a spectacular bed of red poppies like a breathtaking Monet. What a magnificent sight, my partner, a fucking flame-haired double agent motherfucker, spreadeagle on a natural flowering ledge, protruding from a 12,000 foot vertical cliff with the Great Pyrenees as a backdrop. God exists.

"Coming, Jabber," as I grab my special knife from the backpack and unravel the nylon rappelling device. "Be there in a minute."

Life is an enigma; sometimes you just never know. Rappelling along the eye-shattering escarpment, the realization of the moment becomes rather amusing. Shakespeare cleverly wrote tragedies and comedies in the same vein, not differentiating the two. The splendor juxtaposed over the calamity of the situation simultaneously and transparently emerges as an exquisitely stunning contradiction.

How peculiar, to witness God's creations: Earth and man, in such a glorious panoramic dichotomy. Endeavoring to rescue my buddy from a very certain outcome seems suddenly hysterical, not tragic as some would perceive.

Plummeting into the gorgeous, yet out-of-place poppy field, all I can see is red... lovely, blood-red everywhere. Wow, this is mighty fine; what a perfect day to be alive.

Why do I have to kill him? Never killed anyone before, let alone my best friend. Should talk to him first, maybe; perhaps there's a reason—will try to get some info. He may have important names or events: his bosses, turned agents, and his ultimate mission... ya know... shit like that.

Jabber looks so peaceful. I'm aghast. Is he faking? Can't take a chance as I slowly remove my Benchmade Griptilian from its sheath and carefully approach, not taking my eyes off him for a second. I don't trust the fucker.

"You look ok, Jabs. Probably knocked the wind out. Sound much better now," I say.

"You're right," he agrees. "Just stunned. Here, gimme a hand," sticking out his right arm for assistance.

"Ah, before I help you," I offer, "maybe you should purge your soul."

Startled. "What are you talking about, Steven?" he gasps.

"Ya know," I say with disgust, "help yourself a little. Repent your sins, asshole. We can make a deal."

"Don't know what you mean," he replies, baffled.

"Tell me the real story," I demand. "How did you come to this crisis, needing to kill me and the facilitator? What's it gonna get you, fuckface? Why ya doin' this shit, Jabs? Your life will be ruined. Give me some names. Who are your bosses? Who do you work for, asshole? C'mon. Time for retribution. Tell me, motherfucker. Maybe we can help. Perhaps you don't have to be tortured and left here for the rats and birds to eat the meat off your bones while you're still alive. Spill your guts; it'll be good for you."

It's all a game. He'll make his best deal, and we may kill him anyway. Fucking traitor. He was a plant all along. Ha. Small world—we were on two parallel missions, going in different directions. You never know.

Chapter 17

Jabs becomes uncharacteristically silent, not a word—eyes staring out into space. No expression. Then he sighs, turns his head, and looks at me.

"Stevie, Stevie, Stevie. I'm not a traitor, it's just business, my friend. I work for a company that works for a company that is employed by a quasi-governmental interested party. The info you received was planted to deceive you. We are really after the same thing—the control of the asset and his critical technology. Very simple. I'm not here to kill you—merely to monitor your activities."

"Jabs, I thought we were friends."

"Ha, in this line of work, there are no friends… just contracts. I am what you call a master of fulfillment," he brags.

"A real hotshot, huh? So, what's the end game?" I ask him, repulsed.

"To protect the asset at all costs and to make sure he's delivered to the correct P.O. box," Jabs nonchalantly declares and shrugs his shoulders. "That's my job, Steven; my assignment, my contract. Do you think the U.S. government would assign a novice like you to bring in an extremely high value defector... one of the most important prizes in years? Do you really think so, Stevie?" He inquires and smirks.

My gizmo rattles abruptly as more shit comes in. Wow, this new intel reports Jabber's folks, who were arrested yesterday on suspicion of treason, just cashed out. Cyanide. How the shit did they get that? Thought his dad was gone forever. Wow! Maybe I can use this interesting tidbit. Hmm.

"Hey Jabs, ya know what?" I ask nonchalantly. "Your long-lost daddy just whacked your mama and then himself in a very restricted federal detention center reserved for traitors and terrorists. Both are morte," as I slowly take my finger across my neck. "Whaddaya think of that, big shot? Y'all employed by the same company? Maybe you should get a new job."

He doesn't even react—just goes back to his cold stare for a few minutes and says nothing. It looks like he's in a different zone when he shouts, "Fuck them. I'm an independent contractor. They were idealists—didn't see the big picture. They dedicated their lives to the old Shah of Persia. When he was overthrown, my parents became exiles of the new Iran. Enemies of the state."

"So, what about you?" I ask.

"Businessman," he says, almost proudly. "I'm a professional; will work with anyone who pays me, an independent contractor. Don't take orders from anybody or any fucking country. Make all my own decisions."

He looks at me as if to say, 'What did you expect?' And he would be right to ask. Must've been so blind to this backwater Georgian freak-job who wanted to be my friend that I failed to see through his façade. Damn. I should've known... was in denial.

"Wild, huh?" Jabs chuckles. "You never know, just like the old saying, 'Keep your friends close and your enemies closer.'"

"Exactly," I answer. "So, who are you? My friend or my enemy?"

"Both, you fucker. Don't you see? I'm sort of a triple agent," he replies. "Just like in Ayn Rand's book, *Atlas Shrugged,* where she wrote about the military-industrial complex. Well, it has come to fruition. This is the new reality. There are no longer countries, only conglomerates and power brokers. They control the world and people like us."

"What the hell are you babbling about, Jabber, lying there talking about a frickin' book? You're nuts—totally wacko," I state clinically.

With that, he starts to chuckle, then to laugh hysterically.

"Oh Steven, you're just so naïve, no clue about the real world," as he starts to move a little and stretch out his legs.

He certainly isn't paralyzed.

"Feeling better now. Probably just got the wind knocked out of me," he says.

Holding out his right arm, he sincerely offers, "Steven, help me up; think I can walk ok. Just stunned... I'm good. Maybe, ah… maybe we can come to some type of an arrangement—strictly business."

Watching his every move, my vision becomes slo-mo. I locate the baseball seams spinning on the knuckle ball, always unpredictable.

"That's great news, coulda killed yourself falling down here. Thought you were dead," I tell him emphatically. "Gotta be more careful, Jabs. Sure, yeah, we can negotiate something like the politicians do. Let me help you," offering my left hand for assistance but simultaneously watching the seams of the baseball spinning in super slow motion. I'm ready.

Grabbing it and easing him up carefully, my right arm— shielding the knife—explodes from behind and sticks him to the hilt in his solar plexus, ripping up just like they taught us, hearing his sternum pop.

"Love this fucking blade, Jabber, and ya know what? Hated that book; read it in high school—didn't like the teacher, either." I tell him. My voice relays my disgust.

Eyes wide open, staring in disbelief with big red bubbles dropping out of his mouth, Jabber isn't gonna be talking anytime soon.

"So, Jabs, sorry to break the news to you," telling him almost apologetically, "but my name is now Jabber. Ha! That's correct, asshole. Your mother's ugly and your father is a piece of shit, but I'm still your best buddy. As dey say, you done been busted."

The poor fuck keeps staring at me, not comprehending. He will understand shortly; he's trying to talk. All that comes out are bubbles—lots of disgusting, red bubbles. First big bubbles, then little bubbles. Now... no bubbles.

Fuck him. He always said if he couldn't talk, he'd die—very prophetic. Observing his deteriorating status, I want him to know he is a dirt turd and a scumbag, and if the fetching bed of poppies had not intervened, I would have found another way to take him out.

"Jabs, ahm so sorry but there are greater powers that have chosen your outcome. As you said, 'Strictly business.' Love you man, really do." I tell him with a strange affection. "Fuck you, Jabs!" twisting his neck 360° to finish the kill, hearing the gristly snapping of his spinal cord.

He is now looking straight ahead, but his face has taken a complete circumferential journey of the magnificent view—not a bad way to go. Sounded very sinewy, like a Buffalo chicken wing being ripped apart. Yikes.

Man, this was too easy; I actually enjoyed it. Thought it would be the toughest thing to do. This was nothing. My first kill, and it was my best friend forever. That was the moment I became a real Army Ranger. No fear. No phobias. Can do anything now—trying to hold back the puke and the tears—not a novice anymore, motherfucker. You turned me into a professional. Thanks, buddy. Thanks for nothing!

I begin preparing the transformation kit stored in my backpack. It's part and parcel of every op. Unwrapping the special carbon filaments that prevent X-ray invasion, I initiate a series of surgical preps that will render Jabber unrecognizable.

Should've been a surgeon. Love this shit. Dismembering and preserving retinas are difficult, even under perfect conditions—which these are not—like shucking oysters out of the shell. Fingertips peel off easily and remind me of orange rind with a little blood. Somewhat barbaric, yet boring.

I am reborn.

After securing the specimens in an airtight formaldehyde receptacle, I swab his mouth to separately maintain his DNA.

The crunching sounds that permeate the crystal clear air remind me of Beethoven's Fifth Symphony—the extraction of all his teeth to prevent a forensic dental analysis. The heart has already stopped beating, but there is still a lot of blood oozing from his oral sockets. Ugh! Good thing I passed on the local cassoulet, although this is the most fun I've had in a long time. I'm casting his teeth in every direction. Dog tags are removed, safely thrown over the side. In reality, nobody will ever find the body. Vultures and mountain rats will complete the process. Perched on a blossoming bluff in a luscious cradle of poppies for eternity, curiously, Jabber's preserved prints and retinas will keep him alive to his evil handlers and their sick world.

"Adios, motherfucker," A perfect eulogy. It's a beautiful day indeed... as I prepare my exit and wave to the recently departed Mr. James, the Jabber.

The next problem is the handler. Not 100% certain of his loyalty considering my discussion with Jabs. Certainly, the business of facilitation generates huge money. A broker doesn't really care who wins as long as he gets paid and survives. You might say he is an arbitrager, a risk-taker who expertly manages the risk/reward ratio by not picking sides based upon politics—only payoffs.

Allegiance is only skin deep. The scent of money is intoxicating.

Chapter 18

The bosses are notified immediately about the termination of my former partner and the transformation protocol I performed on his body. What is not revealed to them is the informative discussion with Jabs concerning his other employer. That can all be passed on at a later debriefing. Common sense dictates that I should control the dissemination of any new details and keep my lips zipped.

They tell me to await further directives.

Got it.

The next order of business is to vacate the premises ASAP. There is no need to wait around and watch the critters devour Jabs bit by bit. It's going to happen regardless. Nature's way.

For me, the caves are waiting.

My exit pass—Jabber's biometrics.

Satellites and drones. The whole world is watching, just like in the 1960s riots. They're observing Jabs for the time being, but that camouflage won't last forever. Hopefully, by the time his business colleagues figure out what happened, the defector will have been secured and long gone.

His Oakley shades are a combination downhill racing/top gun

mean-ass motherfucking cool. To add to the chic, they possess a bright, orange-mirrored luminescent coating that's visible from a great distance. Jabs said the glasses were a chick catcher. The camouflage-colored bombardier hat, sort of a *Snoopy* rendition is the chick-keeper. Jabber's outfit is so distinctive it should catch everyone's eye—and buy me some time. As long as his employers think I'm dead, I've got a decent chance to carry on with my business.

Retracing the previous route is dangerous due to the likely contamination of my cover, but there is just one train leaving the station—the big hunk of rusty metal I adore. Developing my own departure scenario is essential for self-preservation. Being a hero is great; being a living hero is even better. Locating a safe haven until directives trickle down is imperative.

Immediate clarification of my near-term responsibilities is needed. Being alone in this strange new environment is disconcerting enough, but the lack of transparency is a real challenge. What is certain: I don't have any friends, just killed the only one I had. What's next? Don't know.

Chapter 19

Remembering that you are going to die is the best
way I know to avoid the trap of thinking you have
something to lose. You are already naked. There is
no reason not to follow your heart.
— Steve Jobs

Packing up the shit is easy—it usually is. Remaining clandestine will be difficult. I secure the new backpack "accessories" and retrieve my gear. Vertical extraction proceeds uneventfully, despite the altitude. Training pays off. So does athleticism.

Saying farewell to Jabs is a mixed bag emotionally. On one hand, he was a friend, my BFF, on the other—a scum bag who needed killing like a cockroach ready to attack the cookie jar. Terminating the first roach is easy, but knowing the next skulks just around the corner is very disconcerting.

Releasing the mooring stabilizer and recoiling the nylon rappelling device finally puts the poppy field behind me. Awaiting mission directives allows me to gather my thoughts and assess possible scenarios. Although merely a marionette—albeit now a finely tuned extermination machine-puppet—establishing validity and permitting authentic control of my strings is imperative.

Differentiating between Jabber and me is everybody's dilemma— including mine. Mister Zeman, the bad guy and leader of the Iranian terrorists who desperately wants the defector, will certainly be in touch.

Continuing on the switchback trail is not in my best interest. The challenge is to outguess the guessers. As the intensive Ranger survival training methods were ingrained in us, I can now follow the mantra, 'Don't be predictable!'

Jabs could have been a lone wolf on a single subcontracted mission, but until I learn otherwise, I will assume there could be others. Additionally, Garf Zeman's boys will be coming hard. Formulation of random exit strategies is first on my agenda.

Making myself scarce is my primary focus right now. No better place to look than the hundreds of caves nearby. Attempting to gain more altitude will put me in the clouds and fog—far more treacherous but will also make it difficult to see me.

Until the defector's location is disclosed, my main responsibility is keeping my body intact and getting rest. There will be plenty of action ahead. I am looking for reasonable areas where I can gain verticality.

A simple rope climb technique taught in the Cleveland Heights High School Phys Ed class and repeated during Ranger School elevates me quickly and safely; lock the rope with your ankles and get up any way you can.

...can still hear Coach Kilgore barking at me, "Get the fuck up the rope, and don't come down until you fall." Not sure if he was kidding or not, but I survived and became an excellent rope climber.

Tossing grappling hooks for stabilization, I'm able to climb about 300 feet per hour. Thanks, Coach, you asshole. He would be so proud of my agility and conditioning.

It's foggy.

The twilight topography projects peril everywhere—danger of falling at every turn, slippery rock formations, and violent winds. The combination is deadly. Mixing the joyous harmony of the impending sunset with its comforting blanket of security will hopefully allow me to locate a previously uncharted cave nearby, bed down for a few hours, fortify, and regenerate for what will certainly be a difficult day ahead.

My advantage will be to embark before dawn, rely on my ability to traverse the terrifying geography in the dark, and get the fuck outta here before anyone starts looking. The problem is to find a frickin' hole in the mountain. There are hundreds; they're just not here.

I'm heading east when a brief gust of wind blows some foliage aside. That moment in time reveals an enchanting grotto, beckoning me to enter her. I wouldn't have seen the entrance had I looked one second earlier or one second later. How about that for a chance meeting? I could discus that very deep topic for days.

It's love at first sight, this cave and me—a match made in Heaven. Unabashedly shy, hiding behind a row of glorious cypress trees and wisteria as if waiting for her much-anticipated lover, she welcomes me to the security of her earthen bosom, and draws me in. Entering just as the last vestiges of the setting sun slump below the adjacent western escarpment, I thank God for this timely blessedness.

Chapter 20

There is no such thing as a coincidence.
— Multiple authors

The cave preceded my arrival by about fifty million years and offered refuge to innumerable creatures, including early human beings over that time span. The thought made our chance meeting seem even more astounding. Settling into her life-comforting womb and adjusting to my glorious, yet temporary home allows me to take advantage of her security.

This is a small cave by anyone's standards. It meanders away from the entrance and is difficult to navigate because of the low, overhead rock formations; it gets to a point where I can't stand upright.

Using my flashlight to find possible sleeping areas, I choose a perfect spot behind a large rock. It will camouflage my presence, but offer a direct view of the entrance and anyone or anything that violates her sanctity.

Satisfying my voracious hunger is difficult, but having Jabber's MREs in addition to mine certainly helps. Sucking down a local brew and chowing down on a cassoulet will not happen anytime soon, but I can imagine it. Saliva, dripping out of my mouth—the best beer I've ever tasted.

Exploring the cave reveals the remnants of previous inhabitants. There are a few broken pots that were probably used to cook an unlucky goat. Many of the Pyrenees grottoes were home to prehistoric human beings.

I remember this from my anthropology class at OSU: there are some striking and well-documented cave paintings in many of the larger grottos at lower levels. The drawings, some in dramatic color, captured life at that time. Sienna, maiden plants, and gum and ash trees created vivid kaleidoscopic pigments still used today. Ochre, manganese, and quartz generated a vast rainbow of possibilities. Much of the art is pictures and engravings of animals like reindeer and horses—so important for survival.

My current dwelling has just one simple stick figure drawing of a small animal. The cave is too confined to offer sanctuary for a large group, and it's very difficult to traverse the adjacent area. Indeed, it's perfect for my needs.

Next time, maybe I'll find a fancier cave with some major artwork and pictures of prehistoric naked women.

Chapter 21

...settling in to grab a few ZZZs when Jabber's monitor goes off. Finally, some chatter from the dark side.

I respond to the evil offering using Jabs' forefinger to legitimize my response. Essentially, I am Jabber to all interested parties until further notice. Eventually, everybody will figure it out. *My people*, whom I trust for the time being, may have been compromised by two-faced, motherfucking moles for all I know.

Our side knows that my partner was terminated; Jabber's unknown company does not, and neither do the Iranian extremists. In essence, a business communiqué from the contractor to Jabber would give me a Caller ID to which I can respond. These *Dick Tracy* gizmos are capable of virtually everything—imagination being the only limitation.

Not entirely sure who my friends are, but positive that the Iranian folks, maybe even Zeman himself, lurk behind stealth characters and coded messages. In addition, the tiered inter-company complex that Jabs referred to may have other subcontractors around, all of whom would be extremely interested in the defector. Enemies imitating friends somehow surface like cream in a latte and always have the biggest smiles. When shit happens, reality rears its ugly head and educates you quickly. Sometimes, heartache—even death—is the almighty teacher.

In the world of trickery, treachery, and double agents, you must assume that the other guy knows more than he's saying. There's no way in Hell to totally conceal a high-value asset defection from one of the world powers. It's impossible. Whatever information this Russian is bringing with him must be of the highest level.

Jabs was right when he questioned our status on this mission. Makes no sense. Truth is we are fucking novices; no way around it. Zero experience, but I'm a deep thinker and never take no for an answer. You know what? I'm going to spoil everybody's party and bring this guy out of the dark. Fuck 'em all. They don't know who they're messing with. I'm a freaking master of the universe and a badass killing machine.

Generating believable communication requires verifiable origins: bona-fide fingerprints, retinal scans, and legitimate encryption. Jabs and I were prepared for any possibility and subsequent retribution. It's a multi-tiered platform, requiring each successive layer to substantiate and legitimize the previous level with no party having the complete message until the end.

It works exceedingly well. Multiple messages are generated through complicated logarithms to expose any possible corruption. At the conclusion, if no variation is detected, it's deemed a legitimate communication. Conversely, if protocol collapses, it becomes easy to vet out and terminate the scumbags. It's like a life-and-death video game with most ultimate consequences.

Electronically, Jabber codes to his caller requesting the next order: "Requesting Act II. As per your command, the star of Act I is under the weather and will be unavailable to perform. Request verification and further instructions."

The dark side, either the radical Iranians or a private contractor, immediately chirps, "Verified. Take out facilitator, repeat—terminate immediately. Verify communication and understanding."

Jabs responds, "Roger; looking forward to Act II."

Chapter 22

Trust yourself... You know more than you think you

do.

— Benjamin Spock.

The fact that Jabs and I were hooked up as a team smells rotten fish fishy. Why would our COs do this? With all the shit that's going on in the world right now, coupled with the importance of this mission, who would make this decision?

Very troubling.

So naturally, this latest transmission piques my interest. After hearing Jabber's instructions, my first impulse is to contact my superiors and share this newfound information. My gut tells me— Whoa! hold on, big fella. First, know your friends; then you can determine your enemies.

So that's the issue—whom do you trust? My CO will need to hear from me soon because it's extremely important info I can't withhold too long. The question: Do I spill the beans now, not knowing who is monitoring the chatter? People do the strangest things.

When in a quandary, sometimes it's better to lean back, take a deep breath—and say, "What the fuck?"

Eventually, I'll have to emerge from my cave and establish communication with my leaders, one of whom may be compromised. There's no other way to explain the bizarre pairing of Jabs with me. It just doesn't make sense that they would send two neophytes as the lead intercept team—unless that was their intention.

Maybe Jabs wasn't a greenhorn after all, and I was their sacrificial lamb. Anything and everything are in play. There are seemingly multiple layers of activity with little or no correlation—but now—a whiff of quasi-CIA essence. Being a pawn in a greater game is not my idea of a kickoff to an illustrious career.

At some point, the intrigue will crystallize, and my personal agenda will require self-generation for self-preservation. Like the *Bee Gees* song, *Stayin' Alive* is now my mantra. Maybe I'll even catch the big fish and win the booby prize.

After a limited REM snooze, I wake to the sounds of cave bats returning from their nocturnal adventures. Dawn has not quite presented herself, although there is a faint easterly hint of our great star emerging from her duties across the Mediterranean—the sun.

Before daybreak, I need to get as far away as possible and make my way to Lorp-Sentaraille as originally directed. There are no apparent drones in the area. Monitoring with night vision optics will be very difficult because of the dense forests and lack of any realistic reconnaissance access.

Additionally, heat detectors will be unreliable because of the extreme distances and a myriad of animals such as wolves, goats, and wild boars. Topographically, the shortest range that provides straight-line visuals is twenty miles and requires extremely sophisticated mobile detection technology.

"It's all yours—thanks for the memories." I wave to the bats.

Chapter 23

The Road Not Taken

Two roads diverged in a yellow wood, and I—I
took the one less traveled by and that has made all
the difference.
— Robert Frost

Withdrawal from the sacred, sanctity, and security of my guardian yields a very unsettling and exposed state. Imagine how a newborn feels sliding down the chute of life and entering a terrifying and totally unknown world. Slowly and with trepidation, I emerge about two hours before daybreak and head east along the lower escarpment to avoid wandering eyes.

The dense foliage and obliterating fog provide great camouflage, but it's extremely slippery and I can't see shit. Not a good combination. At every turn, the chances of falling off a cliff are greater. Shit. Gotta be extremely careful—need to get below the cloud line or could wind up like my ex-partner. As the fog develops, sharing this spiritual awakening with Jabs' remnants epitomizes the perfect soul-grabbing moment.

Can't see shit, but neither can any satellite. The early morning air drastically cools as it approaches the dew point. The resulting condensation creates a very precarious situation but enhances my security. A double-edged sword. Reminds me of trying to navigate midwinter sidewalks in Cleveland, singing Paul Simon's "Slip Sliding Away."

Walking to school every day gave me the opportunity to hone my skills in managing precarious icy conditions. To survive intact, I became an expert. Hey, we all played hockey—with or without skates. The slick slopes of the Pyrenees are no dealbreaker for a kid from Cleveland Heights.

With that vision entrenched, before dawn reveals herself, I clod-hop to the adjacent plateau, trying not to kill myself—hopefully choosing the best less-traveled road.

For better or worse, we're outta here.

Chapter 24

The path is barely visible; fog and dim light offer no help to this reluctant traveler. On the other hand, it gives me comfort knowing that, for a while anyway, I can't be tracked. Making as much headway as possible during this segment will allow me to proceed later at a slower and more careful pace. After a few hours, the morning sunrise makes her presence known as my buzzer shouts, competing with the new day:

"COVAC respond and verify."

"ROGER," I reply.

My commanders order me to rendezvous ASAP with the facilitator who has intimate knowledge of the defector's location. HIGH VALUE ASSET—time is of the essence.

Their instructions:

"1st: Take Road D523 south 4 km to roundabout near cemetery. Proceed to the tiny mausoleum in last row; locate an eyeless doll sitting in a rocking chair. Wait for a soft whistle from facilitator.

2nd: Verify knowledge of new EARTHEN code# with alleged facilitator.

3rd: Terminate individual if wrong retort—verify and respond."

"Eyeless doll?" I ask, astonished.

"ROGER that. Yep, looks that way. Oh, and by the way, her name is Cindy," they say.

"Could you verify that?" I ask.

"Verification is positive."

"Roger that. Out," I end.

What am I gonna do with Cindy?

Chapter 25

Sometimes the road less traveled is less traveled
for a reason.
— Jerry Seinfeld

Locating the mausoleum will require a different road than what they suggested. Time is critical, but so is my ass. Not that I don't believe the previous message, but it was generated from a control room by some asshole staring at a navigational system monitor.

The alternative route has better cover and heavier tree density; it will take longer, but it's much safer. The real decision is my gut feeling. The other way is too obvious; doesn't seem right.

Ultimately, I embark on Mr. Seinfeld's Road, not that there's anything wrong with that; it offers the best chance for survival. My façade blends in perfectly; I look like all the other adventure-seeking assholes.

Daylight starts to creep in as I descend to the lower levels. Bits of sunlight appear and begin to dry the paths. The dense fog dissipates slowly and enhances visibility—a welcome reprieve. The enchanting little town of Lorp-Sentaraille emerges from the clouds below me—a magnificent sight.

Trekking becomes less dangerous so navigating the remaining switchbacks is quite easy. I arrive in the town square three hours later, hoping to find a place for lunch—I'm starving.

Nourishment becomes my number one focus. I notice an enticing but out-of-the-way tavern with a sign reading *Bonne Nourriture*, —French for *Great Food*. After all, how many MREs can a growing boy eat?

Perfect joint—a bit of saliva dripping from the corner of my mouth.

Entering the somewhat low-lit establishment, I feel very safe. There are several small tables in the dimly lit back that beckon me. Sitting at an angle that provides a view of all movements gives me even more comfort. The final coup de gras is staring at me with the most enchanting eyes I've ever seen—dark brown poppers that sparkle with warmth and serenity. Along with her eyes comes a face to launch a thousand ships.

Is this real?

Her precisely shorn, French-cut black hair is on fire with radiance and precisely draped to the nape of her neck. Not to be outdone, her flawless skin boasts a healthy olive glow. She's spectacular—and I haven't even seen her body yet.

"Monsieur, how can I help you?" in English, with a sultry French accent.

"Wha... what's your name, young lady?" the words come stuttering out.

"Kassi, Monsieur. What do you call yourself?"

"Steven, my name is Steven, but how do you know I speak English?"

"Ooh, so sorry, don't mean to offend Monsieur but—but you look American—it's ok. You are so handsome."

"Well, if you say so," I respond with a smile, like I'm posing.

"Oui," she says.

How would she know I'm an American sitting here in a little village in the middle of nowhere? It doesn't compute—except... I want to sleep with her.

"What would you like to eat, Monsieur Steven? How about some of the finest, delicately prepared cassoulet along with a local white wine from the valley? You will embrace the succulent flavors from the area, eh?"

"Your ability to read my mind is very intriguing. Been yearning for a juicy cassoulet with goat, turnips, and potatoes, washed down with your wonderful wine. But... I can't understand why you think I'm an American?"

"Well, uh, don't really know, except you look like you play for the New York Yankees," she says as she cocks her head in a very coquettish way.

"Actually, I hate the Yanks; been a die-hard Cleveland Indians fan my whole life," I say proudly.

"Never heard of the Indians, but I know about *The Maid of the Mist* in Niagara Falls. I read about her in school. She's my hero—very brave spirit. Her name is Lelawala, a bewitching maiden of the Seneca Tribe. Anyway, I will now fetch your meal and sit with you while you enjoy your feast; it's very slow. Do you mind?" Kassi asks.

"Mind? Would be honored if such a ravishing beauty would care to spend some time with me," I answer, eyes wide open.

Meanwhile, I notice a guy sitting in the front corner reading a newspaper. He just came in and Kassi never approached him. Wonder why? The man has no intention of eating—merely hanging out—he keeps looking in my direction.

As she walks to the kitchen, I become mesmerized by her best attribute—her long slinky, sexy body. The legs approach each other forming the most scrumptious butt I have ever seen or fantasized. Her waist seems to be at my eye level, supporting a highly-toned upper back with a regal posture—seriously statuesque. Black hair gently caresses her shoulder like falling leaves— breathtaking.

Sauntering toward the swinging door, she momentarily pauses and, with the most graceful of motions—spiritual in nature—turns to me as if to say, "Fuck me any way you want. I am yours." Her deliciously formed, moist lips beckon.

Despite her unrelenting sexual essence, the warm regality of her statuesque beauty and grace is what really captures my soul. At that moment, I become her prisoner—not exactly Army Ranger protocol—at least not in the manuals. Her enchanting eyes undress me as if they were high-intensity, penetrating x-rays. In all my years, I have never seen such a combination of elegance, beauty, and soul—a very scary proposition indeed.

Well, I have to eat something before I cum all over the fancy embroidered linen napkin… although maybe that would resolve the wrinkles in the cross-stitched serviette protecting my privates. Semen can be your best friend—or your worst enemy.

Hopefully, mine will find a home in her esophagus.

With a full-blown hard-on, it's going to be difficult to ingest a meal, carry on an intelligent conversation, or even think straight. Yet it could be a prelude to an indescribably hardcore sexual escapade. Ya never know.

Before I saturate my pants, the newfound dream girl rescues me from embarrassment. With love in her heart and nastiness between her legs, she presents the delicious cassoulet. True to her word, she sits across the table observing my food orgy and silently stares. The recipe is an assortment of the finest local ingredients. The tender goat is perfectly stewed in succulent brown gravy and surrounded with red potatoes, turnips, onions, and a weird-looking green. Warm, homemade bread is sitting on the side, waiting to sponge the au jus.

Man, this is therapeutic. Not only that, but I'm in love with this creature who seems to have come down from Heaven, like it is meant to be. Almost too good to be true, but who cares? She is my fantasy girl. Carpe diem.

"Wow, I'm famished. This is scrumptious, Kassi!" I moan.

"Why are you so hungry? What have you been doing?" she asks, too inquisitively.

"Been busy," responding simply.

"How can you be dat busy and not eat?" she persists.

"Camping out… lost my way," I mutter.

"By yourself? Really?" she purrs.

With a subtle shift of her eyes, she quickly gazes at the other gentleman in the corner. He responds by adjusting his chair.

"Sort of. Why do you care so much about what I was doing? I'm here now," I say.

Her gorgeous eyes pierce my heart—but her inquiry halts. She perceives I'm uncomfortable with accountability.

Don't know if she's leveling with me. Something's not right, but it's certainly not her body. Must be careful.

After devouring seconds and quenching my thirst with a local white Bordeaux, I need to move on or go AWOL—which is not a good idea on my first assignment.

Uh oh. My damn buzzer always seems to go off at the wrong time.

"Where the fuck are you? You're on a mission," my COs are chastising me.

Command Center is getting nervous. So, while my heart, tummy, and dick want to stay, fortunately the gray matter wins out.

"Thanks so much—you are in my heart forever." Hating farewells, "See you when I see you, Kassi."

"Au revoir—maybe our paths will cross again," she flirtatiously murmurs.

Chapter 26

Trust is like a mirror; you can fix it if it's broken,
but you can still see the crack in that
motherfucker's reflection.
— Lady Gaga

Walking out of the café with a hard-on is not easy, but it will give me something to dream about. The sun is sparkling off the incredibly unique street tiles, with hues of blues and yellows calling out to its lucky pedestrians as I make my way to the Vespa store. Getting lost is the next objective.

I've just killed my partner and need to connect with the facilitator, extract the Russian from his cave, and neutralize any bad guys—all by myself.

The first order of business is to proceed to the mausoleum, verify the legitimacy of the facilitator, and, for the time being, distract Jabber's people who want the facilitator terminated. Is there another plot fermenting? What is it? Use my brain. Be brilliant—the whole world depends on me.

Jabber's gizmo is going crazy as if it's having a nervous breakdown—probably should respond to his superiors and assure them. Any new information they give me would really help. I pull the fucker out and set up the parameters for initiating communication. Entering the protocol is easy with Jabber's parts. After going through a series of layered verifications, it takes me directly to the first-tier proxy. That's Jabber's immediate handler, from whom I obtained the Caller ID.

After a series of *Roger* this and *Roger* that, and additional verification sequels like *What is your mother's maiden name*? I'm able to *talk* with Officer Asshole through an encrypted algorithm that provides synthesized oral communication—hopefully without voice recognition.

"This is Horsehead. Repeat, this is Special Agent Horsehead requesting activation directives."

...expecting to get a bullet through my head. Who the fuck is going to respond? It could be another triple-double agent or...?

Initially there is some static, so I repeat my question hoping for an immediate response—more static and interference. What the fuck? Then, after a third try, they answer. Makes me wonder if a tracking protocol is trying to locate me. Shit. This sequence is very disturbing.

Finally, "Attention Horsehead this is XD. There are multiple advisors in the area ready to assist you. Our sincere appreciation for taking down your partner, Officer Steven. The following are your explicit instructions:

Rendezvous with the facilitator and then locate and secure the defector.

Terminate the facilitator and bring the Russian in.

Verify this communication with the previously shunted Special Acquisition Code Response."

Fuck! Special Acquisition Code Response? Not fingertips, retina, but Special Code? Holy shit, ripping his bag apart, *Code, where are you*? —shredding the false bottom. *Where? There, there it is—motherfucker*! on the back of the tissue paper issued for ass-wiping.

Ha, very appropriate!

"***Code#***, this is Special Agent Horsehead# still waiting for command. All directives and protocols have been established and satisfied. Please verify."

"You are verified… Roger that."

I need to get rolling; there's work to do. The mausoleum shindig is about to commence at the end of the roundabout from Road D523. The frickin' eyeless doll will be waiting, and, oh my God—who knows what else?

After renting a sexy yellow Vespa ET4, I scoot out of town, fully fed, totally in love, but not trusting anyone. The *V* mystique, as they say in Italy, has special magic. These enchanting machines make you want to get laid. Maybe it's the seat, the handlebars, or just the aura of the name, but son-of-a-bitch, it works.

Proceeding down the valley on the open road makes me very nervous, too vulnerable for my liking. Finding D523 is no easy matter. No signs—maybe it's a code for something else—fuck. All I really need is to locate that eyeless doll in the cemetery. Stopping in a small, sheltered meadow gives me the opportunity to take a leak and look at the map.

Just as I retrieve my guy for a much-needed pee, the device goes crazy again—happens every time, like clockwork.

Halting a piss in full stream is almost impossible and quite painful—so is getting shot in the head. Making a quick compromise, I switch to a one-finger pee, with a single-handed buzzer beater—not an easy task, and very sloppy.

The device has a quick-alert mode that communicates extreme hazard warnings in real time using lower-tier security without additional biometric verification. It's only activated in hypercritical situations.

The gizmo blares, "Steven, get the fuck out of there immediately—your position has been compromised. Leave now! Return call when 100% safe."

It's the fastest zip-up in history—doesn't even catch any pubes. Man, I jump on the V and hightail out of there as rapidly as an ET4 can go. Vespas are fun and very cool, but not in the same discussion as the fabled '51 Indian Chief Royal Enfield. Now that was a motherfucker, and so was Jon.

Jonny had the biggest balls. There was nothing he wouldn't do. I don't mean robbing a bank or feeling up a virgin cheerleader, the latter being much more fun—but more mischievous or creative pranks.

To motivate Jonny, one merely had to dare him; the caper was as good as done.

Our high school was a traditional-looking edifice with a dark brick veneer that ran about two hundred yards from east to west with the old, antiquated gender-specific entrances on either end. Jonny was challenged to ride his fat fender Indian motorcycle, vintage 1951, down the front hall from one exit to the other. No big deal. Well, we all knew that our pain-in-the-ass principal, who had a rather cantankerous personality, would be very upset. He was also a schmuck and believed his destiny on Earth was to aggravate the BATs. We were at war. It was him against us or, as we saw it, us against the system. We were hoping to torture him enough so that he'd retire—or at the very least, ignore us.

The big day arrived. The entire student body knew what was going to happen. Although they wouldn't admit it, some of the cooler teachers got wind of the upcoming festivities and were fervently anticipating the event with a sparkle in their eyes. It was as if everybody was waiting for the whistle to blow in a championship football game. We were all in our places, ears pricked back, listening for that wailing reverberation of the cycle. The throaty bellow of the Indian Chief was much more distinctive than the Harley Chopper or Hog. They talk about old Harley Sportsters as being mean and ripped—they were frickin' animals, but the 51' Indian Chief Royal Enfield was in a class by itself. Jonny used to sleep with her in the garage. No shit.

Because of the rarity of the Indian, the average layperson was overwhelmed by the scary, almost screaming noise the engine made. That was on the street. Imagine how it would sound in the hard surface confines of Heights High.

My buddy Haddo slowly opened the large oak door on the western end of the building. The prominent bronze GIRLS sign remained above the arch as a memento to the days of yesteryear and sexual disparity. Times have changed!

Everything stopped. Everyone listened. You could have heard a pin drop—or Haddo fart. There was nothing. We waited. Our principal was sitting at his desk with a large coffee in his hand and a scowl on his face, thinking of whom he was going to yell at next. If he only knew what was around the corner.

Then it happened. The most voracious roar that I had ever heard filled the sacred halls of Heights High School. It was as if a thousand lions were singing "Beethoven's Fifth" in the midst of a huge thunderstorm. In the corner of my eye, I could see Jonny at the end of the hall, revving up the mammoth Indian engine. Vroom, vroom, backfire, boom, boom, again and again, waiting for the signal from General Victor.

GO! And he did.

With a screech of the tires and the redlining of the throttle, Jonny took his motorcycle on a journey down memory lane that will never be forgotten. Zero to 60 in 3.2 seconds, from the Girls entrance to the Boys exit, past a terrified administration office staff. The petrified principal screamed in agony at the prolonged auditory assault—and his scream bested the roar of the bike! Can you imagine that? He jerked around in his seat and a full cup of steaming coffee drenched his lap. More agony...

To my knowledge, it was the last time Jonny or anyone else drove a motorcycle through the hallowed halls of Cleveland Heights High School.

Chapter 27

I can't get no…satisfaction.
— Mick Jagger, Keith Richards 1965

My heart is pounding as the Vespa brashly struggles to climb the hill. Sounds like the engine's gonna blow up. Not good, if you're trying to be stealth.

With all this noise, I fully expect to get my head blown off. Anticipation of such an event is scarier than the result itself: because just as you don't hear the lightning that strikes your body, you never see the bullet that emulsifies your brain. A matter of simple physics. The nuns at John Carroll University would be very proud.

Wow! Can't believe—flashbacks now, while facing such dire threats. Near-death experiences can trigger vivid recollections of one's life—usually happier times. Subjects report seeing their entire lives 'flash before their eyes'—hence:

———————

Maybe it was the adrenaline rush, a little weirdness, or both. That was a great summer. My other friend, Jimmy picked me up on his Honda dirt bike and took me to class to study with the Jesuit Sisters—

and learn I did. What a wonderful experience, not only in the physics class but also on campus where some cute little horny Catholic coeds loved giving hand jobs. Maybe it was their way of being friendly, knowing their mamas would kill them if they got laid. It was probably their way of denying sexual relations, a la President Clinton. Perhaps being in the proximity of such a fine Jesuit university made them feel closer to God. Whatever the case, they sure did love to whack the sausage. By the way, I got an A that summer.

Back to reality and for some unexplained reason, Mick Jagger is scowling and wailing in my head, "I can't get no..." What the fuck? I'm on a secret mission with the *Rolling Stones*—hard to believe.

"I can't get no… SATISFACTION!" screaming at the top of my lungs.

Holy shit, kinda lost it for a minute. What are you doing, man? Get your head on straight, asshole.

Taking me out of my zone, a vulture screams by, probably waiting for me to die. Swerving, almost losing control when I notice a clump of trees that hides a miniature cave—a lair. Never would have seen it had it not been for the bird of prey.

Perfect—a gift from God. Shutting down the engine, I wheel the Vespa into the opening. This den will be my home until further notice.

Now that I'm positioned with some level of confidence... who the fuck knows? ...the necessity to communicate is looming. The question is whom shall I call first—Jabs' people or mine?

Easy decision—Jabs' company.

"Horsehead agent awaiting immediate directives," I message to the dark side.

Knowing what the perceived enemy is contemplating before I contact my superiors seems like the most reasonable and simple exercise in common sense.

"This is high command at zero alpha with biometric verification and acceptance," the company acknowledges. "Your performance in Act I was exemplary. Act II will consist of killing the facilitator. He is dirty and cannot be trusted. In addition, we now know the whereabouts of the defector. The facilitator is no longer needed. Repeat, kill the facilitator hiding in a cemetery near D Road 523. Look for a mausoleum with a weird eyeless doll sitting in a chair. Be very careful. Once termination is accomplished, destroy the remains—no remnants of the facilitator can exist. Subsequently, the defector must—at all costs—be brought in alive. Further directives will be forthcoming as to the location."

What's with this eyeless doll?

Chapter 28

I check in with my commanders to inform them of Jabber's new directives. They tell me the facilitator is extremely important and not to fuck it up—I was chosen to complete the mission no matter what.

Why me? I ask. I'm just a young punk from Cleveland Heights trying to get into Delta Force. Why not send your top extraction team? These sovereign countries don't want Americans wreaking havoc on their precious hills and valleys. I have been chosen, they say, because the orders came down from a higher level... Really?

Chosen. What is he talking about? Chosen? Fuck me. Are you kidding? How the hell am I going to bring that fucker in alive with me? This is ludicrous. So, if I were the facilitator, I would be cramming mighty hard, memorizing the special 'earthen code.' Everyone wants him dead except us. Tough business; hope he's getting paid well.

If Jabs' company and the extremists want the facilitator gone, maybe he's not so dirty. It all comes down to the code number and, believe me, I'm rooting for him—I need all the help I can get—a new friend. Obviously, the defector must be one important motherfucking dude. Everybody wants him. This is starting to get as clear as the Cuyahoga River when it's not on fire.

Chapter 29

After the latest communication, it's time to emerge from the den with my cycle. The weather clears, creating a magnificent day in the Pyrenees. Blue skies are dappled with sunlight trickling through the arboretum—a spiritual sight to behold. Vesping along the mountainside to find Road D523 is the next adventure as I scoot the western escarpment, attempting to locate the unmarked byway. This is not a typical tourist rendezvous—today is different. Danger lurks everywhere.

So, who is to meet the facilitator—Jabs or me? That's a very good question. Since the bad guys think I'm dead, it will probably be a good idea for "Jabs," in his very distinctive outfit, to initially approach the mausoleum. If anyone is watching, his appearance will not be conspicuous. Even the eyeless doll patiently awaits familiar visitors, whatever that's about. No surprises are necessary; natural progression is the order of the day.

Descending to the bifurcation of the main path leads to an uncharted geographical demarcation of the route. Take the low road or the high road—that is the dilemma—but no definitive resolution.

Advised to progress on the low road—that's exactly what I'll not do. *Don't follow the herd; it may lead to your slaughter.*

Routing to the long-forgotten byway from the high position allows me to slither through the protective foliage. Finally, D523 emerges. A little broader than I imagined, more like a bigger *C*. European highways are designated *A*, *B*, *C*, or *D*, with *A* being superhighways and *D*, the back roads. This old corridor is not used much in modern times because of the plethora of new intertwining routes and corridors.

Motoring along on D523 creates a tenuous if not false sense of security. Everything seems so peaceful until the vintage German land mine suddenly appears.

I have been told in some past ROTC History of Munitions class that a vast amount of WWI and II unexploded ordnance still exists in France and Belgium. Vaguely recalling some of the images, I decide this one is of German origin—looks like an upside-down tea pot used for outdoor cooking, but this is no camping trip.

It was sitting just off the gravel road. The Germans probably left it as a present during their humble retreat—but if there was one, there could be a hundred.

...may come in handy later, so I remove it gently and take it with me. Munitions training could be very helpful. It's amazing what you can learn in school; the problem is applying it later in life. If I had known that I would be hiking in the Pyrenees Mountains, I would've paid more attention in geography class. Live and learn, I guess.

Getting closer to the cemetery, I hear some engines rumbling behind me. Need to focus. Exposed on this cramped road would not be good, so I scamper into the woods to observe. The throaty purring of the engines sounds like some very high-end vehicles, amplified as they approach.

Nobody travels *Ds* anymore except tourists looking for adventures, bad guys trying to hide, or funeral processions on their way to the cemetery. My intelligence reported there have been no burials for years. It's now just a consecrated ground of remembrance where people come to place flowers and talk to the dead.

Hiding behind some scrub trees and engaging my Steiner 15x80 scope, a powerful instrument that can see forever, I scan all the approaching roads converging on the main entrance. Nothing visible yet, but the noise is getting louder and closer. Sounds like the Champs Elysees in rush hour. Whatever they are, the mufflers are announcing their arrival; multiple vehicles, for sure. Why here in the middle of nowhere? An abandoned cemetery!

Fuck me! Just behind the bend, a ten-car convoy slowly emerges from the trees. Holy shit, I thought this cemetery was dead—literally. There's no funeral, no other people. This is not a sightseeing tour. What the hell is going on?

Chapter 30

Always go to other people's funerals, otherwise
they won't come to yours.— Yogi Berra

Looking closer with the scope, I notice what was not apparent at first glance—identical black Range Rovers with dark tinted windows, but no hearse. Holy shit, this is not a burial—except maybe mine.

Jabs' gizmo burps with new updates, "We have your coordinates. Continue to the crypt, rendezvous at the windmill on the way to the cemetery. If unable to complete your contract, we will intervene."

Jabs retorts, "Roger. Will do my best."

Whoa! Grasping that Jabs' health is parallel with mine and we coexist in the identical metaverse, I suck enough air for us both. Despite the roar of the engines, drones can still be heard above.

My perception is right on—not a funeral procession, merely a caravan of death with lots of observers out there. The mission is being monitored with heavy-duty reconnaissance. Everybody wants in on the action. The defector is creating huge interest.

Securing Jabs' hat and glasses, I reveal myself to the observers, knowing at any moment my gray matter could be roadkill. My command knows the disguise is rigged, hopefully the other guys don't.

Do not fuck this up.

Before the convoy gets any closer, I've gotta survey the rectangular cemetery; it's critical. Nestled in a tiny valley with the foothills of the Pyrenees providing the back boundary, thick woods protect the two sides. The only vehicular access is through the front gates.

Before the SUVs spot me, I quickly deposit my German tin-can welcome gift just outside the entrance. Hello, Garf Zeman!

The classic windmill is off to the side, about three stories in height. It's accompanied by a dilapidated structure—probably an old farmhouse. Part of the roof is missing due to years of neglect and damaging storms with no shelter from the prevailing westerly winds. The windmill's efficiency and strategic location to exploit the gusts were ultimately its demise. In any case, this is to be the rendezvous.

Observing the area, I find nothing unusual. The doors have been blown off; the inside is empty except for rotting roof debris. The windmill itself, battered and almost down, is still fighting for its dignity and survival. An observer can see right through the structure, totally open—no one in there, no facilitator, and no rendezvous. But someone is watching..., can feel it, sense it. *Gotta get outta here.*

Quickly heading away from the structure brings me to a vantage point approximately a quarter mile from the entrance. Scoping the surrounding environs reveals nothing unusual other than the approaching procession. Who are they? Why are they here?

My rangefinder brings me visually very close to the historic but decrepit double-lion archway. Nothing seems amiss, yet everything feels tenuous, ready to erupt—like the calm before a storm.

At one time the cemetery provided a *Stairway to Heaven* for the very wealthy residing for eternity adjacent to the common folk. Led Zeppelin's Robert Plant, who wrote the classic lyrics, would be thrilled... perfect. The affluent stone mini-mansions are in the back, protected by the natural geography of the mountains, while the commoners, with their simple headstones, sought refuge in the front area, just past the gates.

The proud lions guard the main entrance. Certainly, that would be the closest approach, but also the most exposed. There are very few trees protecting the road. The forest on the sides of the cemetery offers more security.

The only safe access is on foot. Hiking through the heavy ground cover on the perimeter, Jabs' hat and glasses give me redundant camouflage. There is no path, just profuse, unkempt foliage amid densely-packed pine and fir trees.

Finally emerging, I find myself in an enchanting graveyard. Several monuments reveal inscriptions from the early 1700s and are unblemished, compared to the many illegible markers. Knowing that people lived here since Roman times offers a ghostly story of civilizations here and gone.

Taking care not to squander any more time perusing the past, I slowly and judiciously make my way to the rear and observe the magnificent edifices that safeguard the dead and their possessions.

No matter the scenario, there will be a resolution of the defector's status. Will I be part of the solution?

Chapter 31

Dolls with no little girls around to mind them were
sort of creepy under any conditions.
— *Steven King, Desperation*

Standing tall in the back of the cemetery amid a sea of seemingly endless headstones are two dozen magnificent mausoleums staring down at the commoners. It's as in life, the wealthy few huddle unruffled in death, swaddled together in their exclusive neighborhood, flaunting their good fortune for all to see. Inhabiting one of these crypts is an eyeless doll guarding the whereabouts of the infamous facilitator. But there is no doll or, for that matter, anything else outside the tombs out of place. Looking closer, six houses of death have windows to peer in or out. Very cautiously, I commence the search for my new best friend.

The mausoleums are glorious in their stately elegance, providing a proper home for suitable people transitioning to the afterlife and beyond... reminds me of the exquisite New Orleans above-ground cemeteries—with little bungalows—some bigger than others. Can only imagine what the occupants' real castles were like. Rules did not exist for these folks. Generally, people of means brought comfort to themselves believing that their most beloved possessions would accompany them in death.

Not knowing what to expect, I feel like a Peeping Tom gazing into the most intimate of settings—very disconcerting.

The first stone cottage contains a fragile antique tea set with some Victorian chairs. The inhabitants probably utilized them every day at high tea in their previous abode—a throwback to a better state of reason and civility. The second house, by far the largest, stunningly lodges a very sad teddy bear and an old train set. The little boy who cuddled with his friend in the dark of night is forever asleep in the back bedroom coffin. I know this is a cemetery, but it's still depressing to encounter dead children—it just isn't right in the sacrosanct doctrine of universal order.

Only six of the twenty-four have windows, and five others are totally sealed—tomb like—never to be violated again by a living human being. That leaves a lucky thirteen with actual doors. Exhausting all the external opportunities to locate the doll via the windows, I come to the agonizing conclusion that my search will necessitate physical entrance into the wombs of these inviolable sanctuaries—not what I signed up for, but duty calls.

Entering the first crypt is a frightening experience—very appropriate that there are thirteen on this Friday, and I'm desperately seeking someone's toy. This is what horror films are made of—or nightmares.

Vandalism and theft are apparent; things look disheveled.

Nothing of value remains: no silver, jewels, or antiquities.

Nobody wants an old doll except me and Jabber's people. Why? What's the connection?

Multi-generational families are entombed in the first six mausoleums: centuries of important people harbored together, enjoying each other's company in their finality. The seventh—lucky seven—is different.

The distinctive gray stone edifice stands out—not that it's grander or more attractive—it's not. It is a miniature mausoleum, maybe a dollhouse, only stone. Everything is diminished; the windows, door, and contents are scaled down to an approximate 4:1 ratio. A minuscule dinner setting with delicate chairs and table ensemble awaits a little girl to serve her guests. Unfortunately, that will never happen. She is fast asleep for eternity.

This has to be it, but where is the doll? Opening the diminutive front door, I slowly crawl through to examine the tiny rooms in the back. Shit—here we go, slinking to the rear, vividly recalling the terrifying low crawl maneuver in the live-fire training drill. Practice makes perfect. The good news is there are no alligators or snakes— can't say the same about snipers who may be lurking. Don't fucking believe this—my first mission, and I'm looking for a doll, a frickin' eyeless doll, no less!

My heart is heavy, knowing this is the final resting place of a young child. Finally reaching the back, a big Ranger like me, a killing machine trained to harness emotion, my eyes well up—I don't want to see dead kids. The tomb of a child is just wrong—heartbreaking and pitiful.

An exquisite eyeless doll stares at me and seems to say, "My name is Cindy—what took you so long?"

Chapter 32

Paralyzed, I can't move. Her sockets pierce my heart as if the Milky Way exploded in my soul.

"I have been waiting for you my whole life," she moans.

Holy shit. This doll is talking but her lips are not moving. Somehow, I'm able to understand what she's thinking.

What the fuck?

"Who are you, little girl? Tell me your secret. What are you hiding? Is there something inside of you? What?" I ask her soothingly.

Cindy is stunning, and extremely precocious. She wraps me up in her spiritual splendor, although she is not the best dresser. Never mind; her innards smite me. True beauty is deeply internal and everlasting.

"Cindy, where is the facilitator? Do you know that person? Please tell me," I plead.

Not wanting to exit the house with Cindy visible, I crouch into a corner, cradling her in my arms—needing to privately harness the power and reveal her secret. Staring into the hollows of her eyeless emptiness, attempting to extract the wisdom, I suddenly realize there is more to this doll than I am embracing.

"What is it, Cindy? Talk to me—where have you been?" I gently ask, not knowing if she understands.

She is spectacular, even for a vintage relic.

Remembering a Shirley Temple doll my cousin had; most models built in the first half of the 20th Century were made of composite—a mixture of glue, sawdust, and cornstarch, and gussied up with all sorts of cute little ensembles. As they aged, crazings or small cracks developed, and like their human counterparts, they often require a little *work* from the local plastic surgeon or *doll doctor*.

"Did someone hit you?" I ask.

Not responding, just gazing into my eyes—she is lovely— limited deterioration and fully intact. Plain and simple, Cindy is a knockout, a ten-plus for a baby doll of advanced age whose dark, vacant poppers hold ominous secrets.

As I draw her closer, she seems to say, "Look inward, Steven; look innermost. Examine your heart. Don't worry, the facilitator will come to you."

What does she mean? Come to me. It's so spooky being in this crypt, but to have an eyeless doll talking reminds me of Chucky in *Child's Play*. Whoa. It gives me the creeps; may never sleep again.

Reminiscent of Modigliani's Portrait of a Young Woman, whose eyes are dark and glazed, as are many of his other depictions. His mantra, *When I know your soul, I will paint your eyes*, permeates many of his famous paintings.

"What do you mean, little girl? Do you know me? ...what I'm

thinking? Spit it out. Do you know the facilitator? You are not really talking, but I understand. Tell me more. Why are you here?" I beg again.

Is there a bomb inside? Is Cindy a suicide bomber?

Chapter 33

Hands trembling, I carefully detach the outfit not knowing what to expect.

Hopefully, her innards will reveal her heritage. Whew. No bomb, but I was fully expecting to discover a French doll company—but now—joyously glaring at me is a tiny label displaying an American flag remnant. What the fuck? This is France—how the hell did a French girl coddle a doll from the United States? I penetrate her hollow eyes, pleading, "Where are you from? Tell me your story—how did you get here?"

"Steven, look in your heart," Cindy whispers again. "Kindness is the greatest form of wisdom, and you are very wise."

Damn. This doll is freaking me out. She's telling me to be kind and I will be all knowing.

Chapter 34

Love looks not with the eyes, but with the mind,
And therefore, is winged Cupid painted blind.
— William Shakespeare,
A Midsummer Night's Dream

Delicately placing Cindy in my backpack, I cautiously withdraw from the crypt to investigate details of her current home. There is nothing—no historical remnants of her heritage or genealogy but this sad little house was built with great affection and respect for both the past and future. The demise of this doll's young friend ripped out the hearts of those she loved. Cindy, in all her glory, was ordained by someone to welcome future mourners who came to pay their respects—or perhaps decipher her blessed mystery.

Carrying around a doll in my backpack is very weird. What does Cindy have to do with the facilitator? I'm missing something—a critical component that ties this whole enigma together. There are so many moving parts on different levels going in different directions. What the hell is happening?

Screaming to the ghosts in the cemetery, "You assholes. This is bizarre—fucking sick!"

Cindy and I reluctantly retreat and carefully scope out the immediate neighborhood. Every placard indicates a French name representing multiple generations of lineage—lots of family members neatly entombed in the closest of quarters. Hopefully, they like each other. Remember, you can pick your friends but not your relatives. Blood is thicker than water, especially *wealthy* blood. Moreover, *royal* blood is even gooier, like Iranian crude oil.

"Where's the facilitator, Cindy?" I inquire, opening the backpack and checking out my new bud.

"So much to tell you, Steven… don't know where to begin," she seems to whisper.

Staring at Cindy, who otherwise has a blank expression, I notice a hypnotic sparkle emanating from her murky sockets.

Drones humming above and satellites afar are certainly observing my actions utilizing the latest sci-op close vision mechanics and orbital telemetric optics. All I can say is, "Fuckin' A."

"We must be very important," I tell Big C, my new nickname for her.

Cindy is far more vital than me. Keeping her alive or whatever will indeed extend my life expectancy. Looking at her neighbors—no Anglo-American names appear on any exposed crypts or headstones, only French. But she's American—why is she here?

I can feel her shaking in my backpack.

"Really, Cindy? You're just too keyed up, escaping from that weird dollhouse. Calm the fuck down. Whoops. Sorry honey, pardon my French," I apologize.

Thankfully, she relaxes—or she's giving me the silent treatment.

Making our way to the left edge of the cemetery, we need to locate the facilitator and take care of business—one way or another—but where is he? Cindy is hiding in the backpack pretending she isn't there, like a little kid going behind a chair thinking no one can see her. Indeed.

"C'mon Cindy, stop acting like a child—I know where you are—I put you there. Where the fuck is the facilitator?" I ask, getting impatient.

Steven, look inward, I remember her saying—but what does that mean?

Inward? In what, her eyes, her soul, the frickin' stuffing? Maybe she means for me to look internally—to search my innards Think... asshole. Where is the facilitator?

Chapter 35

As if on cue, the stone portico explodes over my head, interrupting our peaceful interlude. "Fuuuuuck!" There's a second tremendous blast as we immediately dive to the ground behind the nearest crypt while the third shot tears a hole in the adjacent tree. Where's this coming from? The SUVs? Not the drones.

There's no other noise except the sonic booms arriving way after impact. The speed of sound is much slower than light, like hearing thunder after seeing lightning. No doubt, this is a high-velocity rifle from quite a distance. More than one shooter, different angles of influence—but who? And—*why*?

The fundamentalist Iranians employ excellent snipers; we should have been dead by now. These are not sharpshooters unless they're just trying to scare us. It's possible they want to terminate Cindy, but C isn't really alive—or is she?

The ordnance from these high-powered weapons produces an impact more like an explosion than a penetration—not a pretty sight, especially if you're hit. Muzzle velocity greater than 3000 feet per second could literally blow off a head. *...need help quickly or it's curtains for all of us.*

The monster guns are on fire, spitting out hot lead and rumbling forward to eradicate their intended target.

"AHHHHHH!!!" A second tree is cut in half. If they strike me, there'll be no pain, because I'll cease to exist in my present form. You never hear the lightning that kills you.

There're multiple origins of assault—everything around me is exploding. Never been in a real gun fight before; just the live fire drills in training camp, which were scary enough—this is on a different level.

Ha... reminiscing about my grandfather, a gunrunner for the establishment of the State of Israel. He was a baby clothes/furniture/toys storeowner by day. At night, my Poppy smuggled weapons across the border into Canada—makes my heart sing. Wow, what he would've given for one of these bazookas.

Grandpa didn't give a damn about the type of gun as long as it could kill the frickin' Arab attackers. Most of the weapons they acquired were dilapidated arms discarded by the world's armies. If some of those radical generals had only known that the burgeoning new country known as Israel would be using these weapons to kill Jew-haters.

Most of the guns they assimilated required do-it-yourself volunteer gunsmiths. Lots of Jewish guys and girls became instant munitions experts out of pure necessity... who else would do it? They had to learn on the fly; it was a matter of life and death for the new state and its people. They did whatever they had to... failure was not an option.

I could hear him now, "Sonny, vut du need a fancy-schmancy gun for? ...just kill dem vit vun shot like da boychik David in da Bible."

My grandfather wasn't afraid of anything except maybe my grandmother, but that's a whole different story. Certainly, he wouldn't want me hiding in a cemetery with a fucked up doll in my backpack. He would've said, in his strong Yiddish accent, "Yer da smart kid—vigure id out—vind a pretty girl to make you happy and den marry her."

Oh my God—Grandpa sold dolls!

Chapter 36

If I tell you a secret can you keep it quiet?
Well, I can. I'm not so sure about Doll Girl.
— Brent Weeks, The Way of Shadows

Munitions exploding everywhere. Rocket-propelled grenades are swishing through the air like roman candles on July Fourth, wreaking havoc all around me.

This sedate cemetery that survived millennia and a dozen wars is under attack. Mausoleums disappearing in front of my eyes; final resting places for hundreds of people in jeopardy.

"We are fucked," I tell Cindy. No response from the backpack, although I can faintly feel her trembling.

This is a multi-pronged impingement on my position. Hell of a lot more going on than just snipers; why so much firepower? It's just me and C.

Debris flying helter-skelter... tree trunks exploding.

Gotta be others around. Who?

Fire raining from the sky. Mortars.

Additional weapons being rapidly deployed from various origins. RPGs and mortars to soften up the area. *Why am I still alive?*

If they want me dead, I'd be a pile of bloody pulp. Who the fuck is generating this carnage?

Getting closer, hardly any sound delay. Even an eight-year-old would know that.

...beginning to question my role in this scenario. Through massive explosions, I detect multiple buzzing sounds—drones—from where? What the hell's going down? Can't communicate—buzzer is jammed. "Fuck!" I yell.

Out of the corner of my eye, I can see movement of the black procession as it physically enters the cemetery through the lions' gate. *That's right, keep coming, shithead. C'mon honey, a little bit more. Perfect!*

The entrance explodes into a fiery mushroom. The first SUV bursts into a ball of fire, flips up in the air, and turns over. *Chaos reigns and I created it… thanks to the Germans. Those Jerries sure knew how to build things that last. Love those tin pots. It feels so good to be the aggressor—to generate a proactive attack. Screw them.*

Hahaha, you motherfucker. Mister Zeman, that was a welcoming gift; special delivery from the Germans and me. Ha! Right up your ass!

The other SUVs stop—deadly silence. Reevaluation time for these assholes as all the interested parties are checking their intelligence. Surely, lots of conversations are taking place. Back and forth, up and down. Everyone must be asking, "How did that happen?"

Pretty cool that a rookie like me could control the action—this is fun and I'm getting damn good at it. Going to make my COs proud. Whoa, got so engrossed in watching my land mine do the talking... didn't notice the other SUVs coming through the gates, driving around their colleagues' carnage. Wish I had more mines!

Incredibly, men stand through the moon roofs holding missile launchers. They're about two hundred yards away, approaching rapidly, but I have nowhere to retreat except deep into the woods—a rather untenable situation.

No way all this weaponry is just for me and Cindy. The Iranians must be expecting someone else. Maybe it has something to do with Jabber's information. Everybody wants this Russian dude.

The buzzing from above becomes more prominent. Don't think they are just flying around on a reconnaissance mission. Serious shit going down; Cindy and I are in the crosshairs.

Need to immediately vacate the premises as in—*quitter rapidement les lieux*—like yesterday—*pas demain.*

Where the hell is the facilitator? How can he give me the earthen code if I can't find him? Catch 22. Maybe he'll find me.

Cindy is getting very nervous—think she senses something ominous. I can feel her stress.

Advancing directly toward me, the SUV convoy with a flank of sniper wannabes are spitting out death ordinance at an alarming rate. The chaps appear confused—obviously they can't see me or I would've been dead by now. Either that or they can't shoot straight.

This can't be their A-team. The starters must be somewhere else. Where? Why?

The procession halts. All weapons cease firing. Their systems are also jammed. Probably trying to reestablish their coordinates, maintain communication with superiors, and figure out what to do next. Not sure what their motives are.

The silence is deadly. Very eerie!

All I can hear is Simon and Garfunkel singing *The Sound of Silence,"* and that is a motherfucker.

Chapter 37

Three may keep a secret, if two of them
are dead.
— Benjamin Franklin, Poor Richard's Almanac

The deafening explosions stop. Everything's on hold. Why? No communication. No blasts. Nothing. Cindy's upset. Can't get her to calm down. She's anticipating something; can't be good. Where's the facilitator? Need to conclude this mission, pronto.

A crazed loudspeaker breaks the eerie silence with a piercing cry. The ghostly serenity is fractured by the wacko terrorist in the Range Rover screaming, "Agent Steven, where is the facilitator? We know your position—produce the facilitator or you will die."

How the fuck do they know my name? So careful with the communication. Wonder if they intercepted any messages, remembering the monkey business on my device—the pinging stuff. That must be it. Could have been hacked and tracked. Shit. Our main system may be corrupt. Going forward we'll only be able to use the upper tier encryption—limited functions, but untraceable. Need to warn HQ.

The voice emanating from the new lead SUV, croaking out

threatening shrieks is enhanced by a distinct Middle Eastern accent. The amplification of his voice creates an echo that conjures up a cartoon-like character. Getting threatened by an animated buffoon— although very scary, seems ridiculous—almost comedic.

After a chilly morning, the sky's a brilliant blue with wispy cirrus clouds. The temperature's about 65°—a perfect day for hiking and biking—not dying. There's nothing like the anticipation of death while in a cemetery—so peculiar. It's like a shortcut to Heaven or Hell. This all seems wrong. People don't go to graveyards to die; they go to attend funerals, mourn other people, and occasionally take pleasant walks—but not to die. It just isn't right—sacrilegious and weird.

The remaining vehicles slowly move forward; they're now about a hundred yards away.

The presence of Big C is the strangest phenomenon. I know she doesn't really talk or tremble, but she somehow transmits her essence to my being. She can't comprehend, but I understand what she's thinking. She's not able to speak, but I hear what she's saying. She has no feelings, but her mindset is discernible. She can't emote, but her unqualified kindness is evident, the highest form of wisdom.

Subliminally, her reassurance is soothing. Can't explain it, but simply having her close truly comforts me—maybe through osmosis or some fourth dimension or altered state.

Ready for you, assholes—come and get me.

It has been studied, modeled, and theorized for centuries. Einstein called the fourth dimension *Time.* Other theoretical physicists, past and present, vigorously delve into the space/time continuum. Currently, it is one of the hottest areas of scientific research. As they say, you don't know what you don't know but certainly, physicists and mathematicians have been attempting to solve the intricacies of this age-old topic.

Maybe, just maybe, Cindy is a space/time traveler. Totally mesmerized by her psyche—she's an old soul and we're co-travelers. She is telling me through some dimension to calm down and look inward... "everything will be okay."

Chapter 38

Everything will be okay.
— *Tim Foust, Home Free*

The black entourage of death halts and a fearsome oddball combination Sumo wrestler/freaking Islamic terrorist emerges. A head-shaved three hundred-pound Schwarzenegger parades toward me with a Russian Saiga-12, the latest and greatest automatic killing machine.

Arnold continues his monster walk like he really thinks he possesses the upper hand—probably does.

Now about fifty yards away, with the caravan slowly picking up the rear—he raises his weapon. I can feel the laser burning a hole in my forehead. The intensity is blinding like the high beams of a truck coming at me at midnight.

"Wow, looks serious, Cindy." I whisper.

"Stevie boy, gotcha covered—relax your bones," she seems to say.

Like magic, there's a flash of light and Schwarzenegger's skull explodes—vanishes. Incredulously, he just stands there not knowing what to do. Blood shoots in the air from the headless body, his life spraying out. Then he collapses like the pile of shit he is as an angel from Heaven appears at my side, Uzi in hand, sexily straddling her military-equipped Indian motorcycle as if she's making love with it.

Oh my God, it's Kassi from the café! Now—she's a gorgeous female combo-version of Rambo/GI Jane wearing black combat fatigues. She just saved my life. What the hell is going on?

"Been protecting you, Steven," she affirms. "We are in this together."

"Protecting? What the fuck?" I gasp with astonishment. "Why are you here, Kassi? Have you been following me?"

"Shh. Wait just a second," she says, holding up her palm to me as bullets are flying everywhere.

"עשה זאת," she says into her wrist. "That's Hebrew for 'Do it.'"

A shooting star, brighter than anything I've ever seen, bursts down from its home in Heaven seeking out justice.

The entourage disappears into a fireball. Puff, like the Magic Dragon—gone, except for black smoke and grotesque SUV carcasses. The sound and concussion blow us backward—ribs vibrating, eardrums pounding.

"Told you so, big boy." Cindy proudly declares.

How did she know? This eyeless doll apparently knows everything.

"Do it again," Kassi utters in Hebrew into her device and motions for me to cover my ears. Too late. Immediately, a second strike—even more catastrophic, disintegrates everything—now total annihilation. Try to imagine NO THING—no space, time, or mass.

"Kassi, who are you? What's going on?" I ask.

"My name is not Kassi—it's Avra."

"From the café? What the fuck?"

"We're partners," she declares very simply.

"Partners in what? Why should I trust you? Who was that guy in the corner of the restaurant?" I'm starting to get annoyed.

"Relax—all good. You and Cindy are with friends—you are home," she says calmly. "Steven, we need to get out of here immediately. These dudes were turds, not their best. Elite Iranian troops are out there," pointing to the mountains and surrounding forest.

Shit, how does she know Cindy? Nothing makes sense.

"Get your cute little ass on my motorcycle," she orders. "You're a Ranger, act like one. We need your expertise. Stop staring at my tits." She walks over to me with her lips almost touching mine. Gazing into my eyes, she emanates heat.

Then she slaps me.

"Get a hold of yourself, Steven. Do you realize that if we stay here, we will die?" she asks. "Then your mission will surely fail. Everything you've done so far will have been in vain. Do you understand me? We need to leave right now."

Everything is spinning out of control. Don't know if it's Jabber's death, an eyeless doll talking to me, or the massive explosions that reverberated through my brain. Things seem upside down, but most importantly, I have a mission to complete… need to find the facilitator and secure the Russian defector. Can't leave now and abandon the operation.

"Hurry up," she screams. "The French go berserk when shit hits their soil. It's impossible to conceal two drone strikes. We certainly don't need them coming after us."

Not fully comprehending the enormity of the situation, I just stand there. Everything is happening so fast. One minute this breathtaking creature was a waitress I drooled over—and now, dressed in her sexy military fatigues, she's directing drones to reign terror from the skies... she wants me to go with her. Go *where*?

"What happened to your fucking French accent? Who... who are you?"

"I am Israeli. Listen to me, Steven. We're leaving *now—together*—on my racer."

"Israeli? What the fuck? Can't leave—need to find the facilitator. I'll get... get court-martialed for sure."

"Don't worry," she tells me with supreme confidence. "Hop on the cycle and get ready for the ride of your life—it's the fastest sonofabitch you've ever been on. I'll explain everything later—promise—this has all been planned."

Planned—what plan? What does she mean? Stunned.

Again, she walks over, but this time she doesn't slap me. I don't need slapping because my enormous hard-on perks me up. Avra's tits gently caress my chest as her lips move to my ear and she purrs, "I am The Facilitator."

The decision to go is a no-brainer.

Chapter 39

Holy shit. Avra almost spins out accelerating down a pubic-splitting hairpin curve as I hold her butt close to me. Déjà vu. It's mighty fine riding shotgun, and in this case retro-ass on another Indian motorcycle.

"Enjoy the ride," she says, looking back, smiling with her delicious black hair probing my mouth.

"Look at where you're going," I yell.

"Looking where I want to go—not where I'm going,"

Reminds me of a book, *Racing in the Rain* by Garth Stein, where the narrator, a golden retriever, tries to instruct his master on how to be a better race car driver. Avra is correct—straddling a kick-ass Indian Racer, feeling my dick closing in on the butt-crack of the sexiest soldier on the planet while catapulting full speed down a breathtaking Pyrenees Mountain trail is a game changer. Things will never be the same.

This new freaking cycle is not my friend Jonny's bike—no siree. Riding this beast is like being shot out of a cannon with rocket propellant but it's still just as cool and classic as the early twentieth century monsters. Avra's model is an exotic military-generated custom Scout decked out in army green with a scabbard for her Uzi—so fucking sexy. It's faster than shit, yet extremely mobile even on these wild turns. What a way to experience the reincarnation of the Indian legend.

Descending from the northeastern foothills, the distant sun begins the last of its predictable journey it has arduously accomplished for billions of years.

The spectrum of visible light permeates the wispy clouds as the moisture desperately tries to ascend the peaks with the soaring ospreys and eagles. The water droplets are no match for the glorious birds as a sheer mist momentarily blankets the thirsty greens. This panorama could not have been made by man alone. Surreal.

The roar of the Indian combined with the rushing wind prevents meaningful conversation, however Avra's silence is therapeutic. With my arms encircling her, I ask, "Are you alright?" grasping the intoxicating essence of her body and soul.

"Just zoned out from the supercharged day—collecting my thoughts—everything's going to be ok." she responds.

We soon approach a valley of awesome magnitude presenting a coalescent perspective of the merging mountains, plateaus, and mesas, peppered with cypress, juniper, and poppy fields. God-like.

Avra intermittently talks into her wrist—most likely addressing the multiple stealth drone operators that have been following us since the hellfire experience.

"Intelligence reports about one hundred Iranian crazies are on the move twenty kilometers from here," she tells me in a very business-like manner.

"Where are we going?" I yell in her ear, absorbing her scent.

"Home,—we're going home," she tells me with certainty.

Chapter 40

He felt now he was not simply close to her but that
he did not know where he ended and she began.
— Leo Tolstoy

Skirting the multi-tier escarpment in a series of cutbacks provides an excellent perspective of the northern plain. The basin offers a fertile depository for the moisture that failed in its ascension over the mountains. Vistas of more than ten miles generate breathtaking panoramas causing me to hug her even tighter.

"Steven… can't wait to tell you everything, but do something about your hard-on. Not really impressive," she points out.

Oh my God—driving me crazy and she knows it. For the next thirty minutes, Avra tames the powerful beast in total silence, perhaps anticipating what is to come.

We descend quickly, the trees changing from robust birch, fir, and pine to stout oak, chestnut, and black poplar. Mistletoe is abundant everywhere. We pass plateaus of red poppies surrounded by manicured hedges of magnificent cypress clusters that appear to be manually maintained, but are merely the product of nature at its finest.

Every so often, lavender pokes through the meandering

foothills with its intoxicating aroma. Adding to the final recipe of sensuality are pinches of jasmine brush, just to keep the olfactory nerves riveted.

Through the foliage, I see glimpses of the river, L'Ariège, winding its way north through the breathtaking plain determined to irrigate the local crops and reassure the thankful farmers. It seems like all earthly wonders are singing and dancing in harmony.

With the beauty around me and this sensational woman between my legs, it doesn't seem possible that I just killed my best friend and witnessed unimaginable, devastating carnage. What a disjunction!

Replacing the spectacular views, a small highway appears in the distance. Cautiously, Avra parallels the road on a much less-traveled, but exceedingly more camouflaged dirt trail. She reverses and circles multiple times to check that we're not being followed, occasionally talking in Hebrew to her intelligence people.

Avra downshifts and the throaty sound Indians are noted for emerges with authority; she slows the bike to about ten miles per hour and surveys the perimeter. After a few minutes in a very dense forest, we come to a cluster of tiny cypress trees in a well-sheltered dale and abruptly stop.

"We'll hike now; too dangerous to ride," she warns.

Switching the engine off, she rolls the Scout into the brush and safely hides it while marking our location with three rocks.

"Avra. What's that big hunk of concrete under those shrubs

over there?" I ask.

She informs me that during the war the Germans built lots of sophisticated shit in these hills for bunkers, weapon depots, and whatever else—miraculous engineering.

"Follow me and don't talk," she orders. "Get rid of that boner; you look like a dog on the prowl."

This woman just came out of the blue, from nowhere—was it by chance or a master plan? We will soon find out. Now, she's giving me orders about my dick. What the fuck?

Meanwhile, Cindy is having a ball in the backpack singing, "Hang on Sloopy," Ohio State's official rock song about a fantastic sexual encounter. How does she know this Buckeye theme song from the '60s?

Chapter 41

We have two families in life. One we're born with
that shares our blood. Another we meet along the
way that's willing to give its life for us.
— Mark Frost, The Paladin Prophecy

Tracking toward a civilization unknown to me, Avra marches onward as if she has a hidden agenda. There is so much to know and remarkable memories to embrace with this complicated woman. I need to engage her past and her present—just can't quell my arousal response.

"Taking you home to meet my family, Steven—never done that before." She chats Hebrew into her wrist. "What's up?" Avra waits for the response then replies, "Fuck you, too."

"What the hell was that all about?" I ask.

"That was Zelig—thinks he's my older brother or something— protects my ass like I'm a newborn puppy. Actually, he's my CO and mentor—taught me everything; extraordinary man—one of the top commandos ever in Israel. He wrote the book—legendary, and old enough to be my father. You'll meet him. He must approve of you; thinks nobody is good enough for me."

"Whoa Avra, we just met; what am I getting myself into?"

"I'll explain everything at dinner... follow me, Ranger," she orders again.

"What about Cindy?" I ask.

"She'll have her own seat at the table, of course," answering me as if asked an unbelievably dumb question.

"Got it, but don't you think that's a little weird?" I say with a smirk.

"Get used to it," she mutters, like the conversation was over... so move on.

We proceed through the natural arboretum and enter Heaven— a wonderful little French country farmhouse surrounded by paradise. A lovely babbling brook, a tributary of L'Ariège, meanders through the magnificent property. It nurtures fields of Monet's lavender and circumscribes scores of acres proudly displaying robust fields of maize, wheat, and greens. Within the estate grow the most perfect vineyards—obviously for personal consumption only—and ordained solely to elevate the happiness level of the prosperous landlord.

Sign me up!

"Do you like what you see so far?" she asks, coyly.

"I most certainly do, Kassi—or Avra," staring at her ass as she just shakes her head.

Off to the side is a classically inimitable and exquisitely unique barn that serves as a refuge for the sacred local families of chickens, geese, piggies, and lambies—everything required for a self-sustaining existence. God's creatures are here—just don't get too sociable because eventually your friends will make their way to the dinner table in one form or another.

Approaching the inner sanctum of domestication, a rather paradoxical object becomes visible—the satellite dish. *Says it all, perfect.*

What is strange, but obviously significant: nothing is visible from the perimeter. Everything is camouflaged—very important, especially if you are hiding.

Chapter 42

Just before sunset, everything under the stars awaits our arrival as if to say, "Welcome back—be safe."

Avra smiles and takes my hand. "C'mon Steven, relax—want you to meet Moishe."

The relative humidity appreciably diminishes during the last half hour, creating a shimmering glaze, nourishing the hearty vegetative species competing for purification and hydration. Every nuance is magnified with dew exploding from the fiery sunset. The grand entrance could not be more glorified—a travel agent's wet dream, and my reality.

Without a sensibility of drama or fear, Moishe utters the pronouncement, "Welcome home, children," gazing at us both. "I've been expecting you, my dear—dinner is in the works."

Avra is jumping out of her skin in total joy as she literally leaps into Moishe's tree-stump arms screaming, "Missed you so much—couldn't wait to introduce Steven, my new bud... who could never pass muster in the IDF! ...nice guy, but…"

"Not bad for a half-goy," he declares, as if he knows all about me.

"Thank you, sir," extending my hand, trying not to waver, but firmly planting the finest grip I ever made—a frickin' grand-slam, home-run, motherfucking grip—while staring Moishe in the eye. "It is indeed a humbling honor to be in your presence. Obviously, you know more about me than I do about you, but my mother is Jewish so I'm really a Jew, as they say in the sacred Law of Return. By the way, I am also circumcised," I add, looking at Avra turn five shades of a vibrant red blush. "That makes it official, I guess."

"Doesn't scare me Steven, as long as it works," she chuckles.

"You're right; we do know everything, as you will soon see. Ha, I like this kid already—stop being so hard on him," Moishe winks. "Good job, now let's eat and talk in that order."

The house is equally enthralling inside as it appears on the outside—perfect French country. The front breezeway welcomes nature and invites guests with an intricate white lattice engaging the ivy. Stucco walls with open windows allow the natural light and a sensual westerly breeze to caress the lucky inhabitants protected by the robust oak beamed ceilings.

If I die and go to Heaven, this will be it—I'm pinching myself to help me stay in the present.

The walls are alive with assorted frescoes illustrating the glorious indigenous way of life. There is also a collection of early framed Monets, probably done while he was a student. Nevertheless, they depict frolicking landscapes exploding with vibrant colors portraying happy outdoor romps. The intensity of the hues, so profoundly alive, has as much to do with the success of the painting as the local scene—splendid.

To the left, I am told, is the 400-year-old family room with a monumental walk-in fireplace adorned with Pyrenees stone and cast-iron sculptures protecting the inner hearth. Understandably, there is no 80-inch Samsung TV ruining the wall—just a stunning fresco detailing the easterly panoramic vista with the enormous defensive peaks framing the fertile plain below. This is the meeting room, cocktail hour room, after-dinner, and any newsworthy-juncture-room. It amiably offers refuge for family and guests to fulfill daily social or crisis-management obligations.

The best part of the house, however, is to the right of the engaging vestibule—The Kitchen—an *Architectural Digest* gastronomical fuckin' A Monet's perfect kitchen. Copper pots hang from the ceiling, sheltering two magnificent oak butcher blocks on either side of the huge white porcelain farm sink.

The wooden cabinets are a distressed light blue wash and obviously broken in for hundreds of years. The floor, which extends into the dining room, appears to be reclaimed barn wood—decorators everywhere would kill for these components. Seriously, where am I? Shaker Heights, Ohio?

The dining area, an extension of the kitchen, nurtures a huge cherry ash antique table. Accompanying the table are magnificent oak armchairs. Chantilly-laced sitting pillows offer exquisite comfort for the lucky inhabitants and their guests.

A flamboyant fella barrels out of my chef's dream room, "Welcome Steven, my name is Raffi, and you are family so you can call me Raf."

"Holy cow, nice to meet you, Mr. Raffi. Thanks, I do feel connected."

He comes over and gives me a big bear hug. Raf is probably my size but extremely wiry and looks like he'd been through a few wars with those big scars on his forehead and right bicep. His wavy golden locks are still intact, and his cherub face is perfect with bright, rosy-red cheeks and an irresistible, wholesome smile. Somewhere, somehow, his piercing blue eyes have seen more than their share of war and anguish.

He nods to the table and says "Come, sit down—we have a lot to talk about. I'm the designated cook because I love to eat—and eat what I love. You're in France, but we're going to have a proper Israeli dinner. However, this is still France, and we will drink the local wine from right out there," pointing through the expansive windows and the vista beyond. Raffi pops the cork. "Bon appétit and, as they say in Jerusalem, l'chaim, to life."

"Hey, wait for me," a musclebound, macho, blond-haired, blue-eyed 'Rambo-guy' says, barreling into the room. "Never miss a meal. Hey Steven, I'm Zelig, Avra's CO and guardian angel—great to meet you." With that, he grabs me, almost breaking my ribs, while whispering in my ear, "Don't ever hurt her—got it?"

"Yikes," I moan. "You guys certainly like to hug around here.

Holy shit!"

"We only hug people we like; you should feel honored," Zelig tells me, affectionately.

"What do you do with folks you don't care for?" I ask.

"Don't ask; you don't want to know," he says, straight up. "Anyway, we're going to make you into a real soldier so Avra will be proud. You need a little work on your confidence and psyche. Don't worry so much—we are extraordinary mentors of winners—the best in the world, as you will see. Your instruction begins immediately—let's eat."

The meal is truly Israeli, starting with Saj, a pita-like Lebanese unleavened bread, rolled with feta cheese, radishes, and bits of mint—indescribably delicious. Next comes the enormous dancing shrimp which, incidentally, are farmed in Israel where both the art and science of maintaining self-sustaining food were developed. The sumptuous creatures, cooked in olive oil and garlic, are served over couscous with sides of humus, baba ghanouj, and stuffed grape leaves.

Those are just the appetizers; the main course is the famous St. Peter's fish.

Raffi explains that the recipe and the species originated in the environs and water of the Sea of Galilee. Normally, tilapia is used, but you can substitute bass or trout depending on the fresh catch of the day. This is a local sea bass from one of the nearby Mediterranean ports near Marseille and was flown in this morning by helicopter, specifically for this special occasion. Not sure if I believe him, but it makes for wonderful conversation.

By the way, my new friend Raf talks a lot—not quite as much as Jabber, but he is extremely passionate about his cooking and many other critical issues, like black-ops maneuvers in the Iranian nuclear facilities. Whoops.

At any rate, the presentation is magnificent. The famous fish is served whole, of course, lightly pan-fried in olive oil, flour, lemon, and garlic, surrounded by a rainbow of local vegetables, a medley of cucumbers, peppers, squash, and tomatoes with a savory tzatziki sauce on the side—scrumptious.

Wine flows. Food is inhaled—a gluttonous eating orgy. I'm fantasizing about what is yet to come. Avra interrupts and sighs.

"Steven, I must tell you—this land has been in my family for over 500 years."

"What? What are you talking about?" Staring at her in astonishment, "Tell me—ya gotta tell me everything." *...need to fuck her one fine day!*

Chapter 43

Life is a journey, not a destination.
— *Ralph Waldo Emerson*

Raffi starts to clear the dishes and smiles.

"While I get everything out of here, Avra can paint you a dramatic 500-year documentary as you munch on this sublime rugelach, my great grandmother's recipe from Latvia. It's like nothing else you've ever tasted. This variety is rolled with creamed cheese, cranberry rhubarb jelly and topped with walnuts—yum. Then you'll wash it down with some real Turkish coffee and a superb Israeli port," nodding to a painting of the Jerusalem Western Wall.

Avra winks at me and begins telling me the remarkable story of her heritage, while Raffi returns to the kitchen and belts out Willie Nelson's awe-inspiring lyrics to "Don't Let the Old Man In," while preparing the next course. It's a very poignant song, considering the mature ages of Moishe, Zelig, and Raffi—their theme song. But before Avra can get very far into her history, everyone's phone blasts a sudden notification like an 'amber alert' or storm warning. Raffi stops singing mid-sentence and calls security... then comes some rapid Hebrew conversation.

"There's been a breach in the first tier of the outer perimeter," he yells as he rushes back into the dining room. "It's in the north end of the property."

Avra tells me this normally doesn't create an alarm, merely a notification to the camera monitors to check it out. Ninety-nine percent of the time, an animal sets off the alert. This is different: a soldier-like individual initiated the intrusive event. If a person or vehicle were able to penetrate the second or next protective layer, that would be a much more serious incident and produce loud hyper-alarm warnings through the entire estate with critical response protocols.

Intelligence reports that the cameras have imaged a single intruder, maybe a lone wolf or a scout from the Elite Iranian Brigade, or possibly a straggler from the ragtag group at the cemetery. We have to find out and bring this person in.

"Thought we killed 'em all with the drone strikes," I say.

"They're like cockroaches," Avra hisses.

Zelig immediately takes command and says, "Steven, you come with me. Let's see you in action, my friend. We'll approach from the east."

Avra and Moishe are told to advance and intervene from the west to create a pinch and then immobilize the person of interest. Ha, just like a defensive football scheme where the cornerbacks and linebackers pinch in to blow up an offensive play.

"We'll find out who this fucker is," Zelig declares. "I would like to bring him in alive for interrogation—but never take your foot off a snake."

It's still dusk, so we paint our faces with black-out to prevent any reflection. Each team leaves separately, departing in designated directions.

I make sure my trusty Glock 19 is holstered; Avra has her Beretta. Zelig and Moishe prefer their Sig Sauer P226s. All have suppressors. As we leave, I feel for my sweet Benchmade Griptilian blade. The others are equally comfortable with their KA-BAR knives.

As we depart, Zelig reiterates, "Take this guy alive."

This is like a mission within a mission. We proceed very cautiously as there may be others around. For the first time, I'm able to appreciate the vastness of the property; we will need more eyes to locate the intruder. Once something passes the outer perimeter, the cameras are not sufficient. We requisition the nearest satellite and send up a reconnaissance drone to assist. Zelig reports getting a positive visual on an individual fairly close to us.

Here we go.

Moishe and Avra are much farther away, so it's our ball game to win or lose.

Zelig and I separate so we can approach this asshole from different angles. Across the grassy knoll, I focus my Steiner scope on him; he looks like a professional with black-ops fatigues.

Stealthily, we zero in. I go around the back, Zelig to the front. Getting nearer; heart's pounding—but this is what I signed up for.

Zelig distracts the intruder's attention by throwing a rock, as I silently close from the rear. I wrap my left arm around the dude's neck, apply a knockout choke hold, and take his feet out with a leg sweep. My other arm holds a knife under his jaw as I say in Farsi, "Don't make a sound or you will die."

Simultaneously, Zelig secures his wrists with plastic restraints and asks his name, rank, and what the fuck he's doing here.

No response.

The fucker isn't talking even after Zelig kicks him in the balls. He has no individual identification other than a green beret with Iran's 65th Airborne Special Force Brigade's insignia, a dagger and golden wing. They are excellent soldiers, originally trained by U.S. Special Forces in the '60s under the Shah's Persian regime. They kept the beret as a show of respect in honor of the U.S. Green Berets and are now called the 65th NOHED brigade. Until recent years, they still trained with the U.S.

Our captive wears a generic black commando outfit and carries a Browning HP pistol and an old pesh-kabz knife. He also has a small earphone walkie-talkie type of communicator, which is useless to us.

We take his picture for facial recognition. Zelig says to take him back, and see how he deals with real pain. He repeats that in Farsi, so the prisoner understands. He also tells him that a female Mossad agent will administer the interrogation while he's naked.

That gets his attention. His eyes pop open, and he screams, "No, no!"

"Well then, fuckface, you're just gonna have to tell us the

truth," I nonchalantly tell him.

He keeps babbling, "No, no." Then he clams up for good—won't even look at us.

"Ok, Steven," Zelig says, "we still have a lot to tell you. Let's take this fucker back, finish our dinner, and have him think about his demise. We'll present him to Avra so he can marinate on that for a while."

Placing a full head blindfold, we drag his ass to the house. Before we secure him in one of the safe rooms in the basement, Avra introduces herself and whispers something in his ear.

The fucker starts screaming and goes berserk.

"Holy shit, what did she say?" I ask.

Zelig just shrugged his shoulders and smiles.

Moishe meets us at the door and gives me a big bear hug. "Good job, sonny boy; you're a quick learner. Now let's have dessert. There's more good stuff for you to hear, but I'm still hungry."

I have so many questions.

We reconvene in the dining room just as we were seated prior to the rude intrusion. It certainly was an interesting interlude before the final course, ha! At the very least, we were all able to go outside, stretch, and exercise a little—but not exactly in the way we would've thought.

After sitting for a few minutes trying to comprehend the severity of our situation, Raffi says, "Fuck those assholes; let's finish our feast—worked so hard preparing it." After that, everybody relaxes knowing we have things under control for the short term. Israelis never really know what tomorrow will bring.

So, continuing with dinner, I think it's a good time to ask Avra, "Why, why am I here—what the fuh—what the fuck is going on?"

"Listen and you will understand," she responds sultrily, smiling. "For 5,000 years, our people have been exiled from more countries than you can name." She sighs and closes her eyes for a few seconds to gather her thoughts. "Every second of every day somebody, somewhere, tries to embolden and rekindle the hatred, ethnic cleansing, and genocidal bleaching—the proverbial and unrelenting holocaustic mindset. Over the years, everyone has attempted to kill us, incinerate our flesh, and bury our culture, but we have persevered. The Romans, Crusaders, and the Catholic Church tried. The lowlife, despicable piece of shit, Adolph came close, but we are still here. My ancestors lived in Spain for many centuries—extremely productive and very happy until they were fucking thrown out in 1492 with the famous 'Alhambra Decree,' the edict of expulsion. Ferdie and his fat-ass wife, Big Bella evicted every single Jew—see you later, Jew pigs."

Avra continues. "Most inhabitants of our town fled and hid in the Pyrenees for several years. Eventually, they settled in this region and thrived for over four centuries." She says and points outside. "My immediate ancestors purchased this very property, farmed the fertile land, and cultivated successful mercantile businesses in nearby Marseille. Through all that, they raised their families with love and education and never wavered from their faith—my family—my heritage.

"Hitler arrived and we overcame," Avra declared triumphantly. "Now we are faced with the biggest crisis in our history; the wacko fundamentalist Islamic terrorists are out to eradicate us and wipe Israel off the map. How do you fight a martyr-loving enemy that is dedicated to our obliteration?" Avra bluntly grins. "Fuck them. We will do whatever is necessary—anything and everything is on the table," raising the glass of port, "לחיים (To life, l'chaim)."

Moishe looks at me and says, "This resplendent abode that has been in Avra's family is now a safe house for our country, a perfect location close to the sea as well as the mountains. Pretty cool, eh? Raffi and I are its part-time caretakers, so to speak, but full-time Israeli black-ops scary motherfuckers. So is your cute little friend over there," he points to Avra and continues, "There is no name for our group because, well, it doesn't exist—ha! But Zelig, that musclebound freak, is the field commander. Everything here is a façade to camouflage our real purpose—the pro-active protection of Israel and its people, at all costs."

Great history lesson, but what does it have to do with me? Everybody is very emotional, and each has their own personal story to tell; all very poignant and extremely motivating. But how do I fit into this Mossad black-ops unit?

Chapter 44

THE PLAN

Some champions are born; others are forged!
— *Kierra C.T. Banks*

"Wow," I exclaim. "...still don't understand why I'm here. Avra mentioned this was all planned. I know that Israel is in my blood and that my mother's grandfather was a gunrunner or something like that in '48, but nobody really talked about it when I was a kid. I know that my father's not Jewish, but my family has always been fervent supporters of Israel—passionate Zionists."

Moishe raises his hand, "שֶׁקֶט shekat (silence). Let me tell you a story—a very special tale, but true. Your great-grandfather and my grandfather were best friends, like brothers, but even closer because they believed in the same cause—the establishment and the absolute perpetuation of the state of Israel."

I can see his eyes moistening and his cheeks flushing. Stunned, I can't imagine what's coming, but before he can continue, Raffi comes running in from the kitchen with new information. "We ID'd the prisoner through facial recognition. His name is First Lieutenant Omar Roosh."

As it turns out, intelligence has a file on him. He's been around for a while. A career officer stationed in France, and part of a special commando unit for operational control... whatever that is. Unfortunately, these assholes are here legally to protect their diplomats and create mischief. He is 38 years old, married, with two kids.

Zelig insists we talk to him immediately. Avra, the sultry Mossad agent, and Moishe, the huge scary guy, will be the hosts. Depending on the interrogation, we can make him vanish or just send him on his way. Certainly, we can't take him back to Israel or turn him over to the French authorities. It would be very difficult to explain our status here.

"Let's offer him some of our delicious food and have a nice little chat," Moishe says.

We all go down to greet our guest and give him a little taste of Israeli hospitality. The rest of us will observe the interrogation while they spearhead it. Avra carries in a plate of food while Moishe follows with some bottled water.

Knowing that he probably won't talk to Avra, Moishe begins the conversation.

"First Lieutenant Roosh, we know who you are. What we don't know is what the fuck were you doing on our property with a gun?

Assassin? Spying on us?" Moishe lifts him up, chair and all, and throws him across the room like a toy.

"Moishe's like a bull; holy shit!" I exclaim. Roosh starts to moan.

Raffi says Moishe's just toying with him, having a little fun.

"You should see him when he's really pissed," he laughs.

Moishe and Avra help Roosh up, brush him off, and gently put him back in his place by the table like nothing happened. The prisoner is horrified but still gives no response when asked the same question.

Moishe continues, "You must be very hungry. Why don't you have some of this tasty food; then maybe you'll be more relaxed and tell us why you're here? Next time I will bounce you off the wall. We can detain you for a long time, ya know. Israel does that shit occasionally. You'll have grandchildren who will never see you. You'll be discarded like a piece of garbage. No one will speak your name. Is that what you want?"

No response.

They remove the head mask and replace it with a blindfold, never allowing him to see our faces. Maintaining his restraints, Avra approaches and tells him very softly that she is going to feed him.

He turns his head away but says nothing.

She comes in closer and places her hair up to his face and slowly moves her head back–and–forth.

"Lieutenant Roosh, doesn't that smell good? Don't you want to touch me?"

"No," Roosh finally speaks.

Not giving up, Avra places her forefinger on his lips and gently massages them until he barely opens his mouth. She then inserts her finger and touches his tongue very gently. The bastard starts to get aroused. Son of a bitch, Avra is good—really good. His crotch starts to move. Hilarious—what a show. I'm getting excited.

She unzips his fly and whispers to him in Farsi, "Why don't I give you a throbbing, juicy hand job and send the pictures to your wife and kids? I'll bet your commanding officer would like to see some pics. So would the Imam from your mosque. You'll be humiliated for life, Lieutenant Roosh."

"Ahh. No. No. No. Please, no," he begs.

Avra tells me to take his pants down but leave his tighty-whities on. Everyone puts on head masks so we can't be identified. She then removes his blindfold and starts to whisper in his ear. He develops a massive tepee that almost bursts through his underpants as Raffi takes a bunch of snapshots for posterity.

"Oh no. No. No. Stop," Roosh begs. "Please no!"

Moishe slams his fist on the table so hard that the plate of food flips up in the air. "Then tell us what we want to know," he screams.

No response.

Putting the blindfold back on, Moishe grabs him by the hair and yanks his head back while Avra sticks the water bottle in his mouth upside down and squeezes the plastic until the water begins to choke him.

"Ok, ok," he cries. "Just get that whore away from me. Now. Now! Get her out of here."

Ignoring his demand, she takes another bottle and slowly drips it on his underwear, further arousing his already massive erection. It's shocking what the human mind can do to a person. The mere suggestion of something can be worse than reality.

"Too bad, Omar," Avra says. "We could've had a good time," she says and slaps his face so hard that his lip bleeds. Then she tips the chair backward until he hits the floor. To add insult to injury, she pours more water in his mouth while Moishe covers his nose. Not a pretty sight.

"Ok." Moishe says. "Enough of that monkey business. Why the fuck were you watching us? What were you up to? If you don't tell us, it's not gonna end well, Omar. We can have an all-night party, and you will be the main attraction."

Roosh sits there for a few minutes, not saying anything, then slumps his head and starts sobbing. Moaning, he finally relents and begs that we keep the whore away from him. Ha, that's his only condition. ...horrible how these radical jihadists think about women.

He proceeds to tell us that they are desperate to get the Russian defector. Although the Russians are their main funding source for terrorism, Iran covets more. They want to be a superpower and control their own destiny—not be a pawn or proxy for Russia. They feel that having the defector would be a game changer.

Apparently, they followed us from the cemetery after we

annihilated their idiot troops. The troops were just a decoy, Roosh tells us. Crazy, they sacrificed all those people... for what?

"We'll do whatever is necessary to accomplish our goals," Roosh keeps ranting.

Moishe goes berserk when he hears that and slams his fist into Omar's solar plexus until he almost passes out.

Wow. These assholes think they can rule the world and force everyone to follow Sharia Law. Their real goal is to destroy Israel. Nothing else really matters to them. They exert terror for the sake of terrorism. Real bad dudes.

"How did you even know about the Russian defector?" Moishe asks after calming down a little.

The prisoner, recovering from Moishe's massive fist, finally responds. "Do you think you are the only ones with spies, moles, and double agents? We invented that stuff."

"Is the famous Garf Zeman your commander? Is he here running this operation? Tell us. Tell us fucking now!" Moishe screams and smashes the table so hard again that Roosh almost falls off his chair.

"Zeman will cut your balls off. You have no idea who you're dealing with," Omar whimpers like a child. "He'll blow up France bit by bit until he finds the Russian scientist. Then he'll destroy the Zionist state and all its children."

"Is that so?" Moishe yells. "Fuck you! We're going to send you back and tell them you spilled your guts."

"Put his head mask on and get 'im outta here, fucking terrorist," Moishe orders.

"No. No. They'll hang me, hurt my children. Please don't—don't make me go back. I'll do whatever you want. Please," he begs.

Silence.

"Ok, Omar, that's what we want to hear—real cooperation. So, pay attention very closely, asshole. We've got a proposition for you that you can't refuse," Zelig says. "In the long run, you will be very happy, and, God willing, you'll be able to enjoy your future grandchildren."

Moishe explains that we own him. He now works for the Israeli military, which will safely archive those delightful pictures.. He will be given details of his future communication protocols with us. His new name will be First Lieutenant Omar Mole Roosh.

"You will be a spy and get the information we need when we want it! Do you understand, Goddamnit? Do you fucking understand?" Moishe screams.

Roosh nods his head.

Avra tells him, for the record, "Just know that I would never have touched your slimy, disgusting cock, but you can still dream about it, you piece of shit."

In the morning, we will release him in the woods after he is prepped for his future job as an Israeli agent. He will tell his commanders that he tripped and got lost and that his earphone broke when he fell.

After concluding our business, we gather back in the dining room.

"Sorry for the interruption; terrorists don't take a time out," Moishe tells us. "As I was saying, your great-grandfather was not only a passionate Zionist, but he was also a zealot. A man of means in real life, owning a children's store, but—in his other life—he was a commander in the U.S. Navy. Can you imagine at that time, a Jewish boychik… commander?"

Moishe pauses for a few seconds to collect himself and then continues to tell me that his grandfather was also a zealot and a general in the Haganah, which in 1948 was really a paramilitary group in Palestine that spearheaded the establishment of the state of Israel. He explains, it became the central core of the Israeli Defense Forces or IDF. Its culture, dedication, and fervency still exist today in the hearts and minds of every Israeli soldier.

I'm getting a history lesson on my heritage... unreal. It's so cool to hear they were ardent believers, sort of wacky like me, afraid of nothing but with this crazy dream—the land of milk and honey—a Jewish State—where Jews after 5,000 years would no longer be persecuted, no longer fear being thrown out of a country for merely being Jewish. There is now a homeland and safe haven.

Moishe continues, "They met and bonded for eternity—soulmates, you could say—your great-grandpa and my poppy—and you and I are the products of their uncompromised friendship and passion of purpose. So here we go, Steven," Moishe declares, proudly.

"Hang on to the seat of your pants and grab another drink! You were born and bred to be the perfect double–agent—you are Rocky, Secretariat, and Sandy Koufax rolled into one. Your sacred and intimate purpose in life has been ordained prior to and since your first fetal scream. Steven, welcome, shalom שלום."

What the fuck is he talking about—preordained? Oh my God! Is my life not real? I mean, if I'm not me, then who the fuck am I? Goddamn Koufax?

Cindy screams at me, "Stevie boy—this is crunch time—grab the brass ring and don't fuck it up!"

Moishe continues the mind-blowing story. "They had a plan, essentially conceived by your great-grandfather and carried through to your conception and breeding. It is no accident that your father was an incredible athlete, and your mother is statistically super-brilliant. Everyone in your family going back to your great-grandparents had an affinity for leadership and character. You were well bred—you just needed proper training like a champion racehorse. This plan to which I am referring—this master plan—was to produce a sacred offspring capable of transparent international boundary movements without detection and having the capability of a super double-agent. Steven, you were born to be a spy, an assassin killer-elite, maybe our eventual leader. You have been chosen for us, Israel, and Avra."

"Yeah... we'll see," Avra chides, "but he does have a cute ass."

"What about the U.S. Army? My... my unit? My... my CO? Going to get court-martialed. Gonna cut my balls off. Fucking AWOL.

Whaddaya—Whaddaya fuckers doing? Get me out of here! Gotta go back to my unit—my people."

"We are your people," Moishe sighs.

Zelig laughs. "Well said. Ha—not the whole army—just your CO's boss, General Cooper Mason. That's right—the good general is truly complicit. Ha, it turns out his grandfather was also best friends with ours."

It's wild beyond comprehension to hear that they initiated this sacred plan while having a few beers and fighting Syrians in the Golan. Sounds like my BAT buddies from high school. They were talking about the future and being proactive, and I am the product of this pure Zionist-loving brain trust. Can you believe it? Can't make this shit up. They're telling me it's fucking true.

"This master plan," Moishe solemnly tells me, "was set forth with love in their hearts, passion in their souls, and the state of Israel as their destiny child. So, enjoy the journey and relish this beautiful and talented shayna maidela," pointing to Avra, "cuz she's gonna be your wife—for real."

"In your dreams," she says, blowing me a kiss.

Chapter 45

To say that I am flabbergasted would be a colossal understatement! It's more like pithed, like when your seventh-grade science teacher tortured a poor defenseless frog and stuck a sharp instrument through his fragile brain stem and then secured his arms and legs with pins and proceeded to eviscerate his guts in front of nauseated, laughing, and pimply-faced adolescents.

Well, I feel worse than that: pummeled, obliterated, and castrated. On the other hand, Avra is freakishly sexy and extraordinarily breathtaking—not such a bad deal.

"Ah… ehm… ehm." Avra demands our attention by clearing her throat, "Ah… ehm… ehm."

After a moment of deafening silence, she slowly begins to speak.

"Moishe, Zelig, and Raffi are intimately familiar with my history, but for your benefit, Steven, this is my story. Let me begin with Cindy—your new friend—your spirit. Actually, she was my grandmother's doll."

Whoa, this is getting really weird!

Avra's eyes glistening, she continues, "My ancestors enjoyed centuries of harmony and peace right here on our sacred ground," motioning to the surrounding environs, "and in this spectacular edifice until 1935, the year my family's lives imploded. That was when the fucking hair-lip began his terrifying psychodrama of taking over the world and eradicating our heritage," nodding to us. "My great-grandparents were exposed by frightened neighbors across the valley and were never seen again. They had four kids—all gone—vanished, except for my grandmother who somehow escaped. She miraculously survived along with her little doll, Cindy—that's right—your Cindy—my Cindy."

Trying to hold back tears, she persists in venting and vomiting up the past. "Bubbe was raised by a poor French farmer and his wife along with their other children. They lived in the foothills of the Pyrenees. She was home-schooled and miraculously escaped the wrath of the obsessed Germans. The farmer was so poor and their lives so meager that the greedy Nazis were not very interested. Despite their paltry subsistence, they saved her life—my life. Somehow, she made her way to Palestine and worked on various kibbutzim and eventually met my Poppy. They were soulmates and very smitten with each other and especially—Zionism—a true love story."

This whole thing is feeling more like a clusterfuck. To have the meaning of your life change in an instant is a mind-blower.

"Bubbe and Poppy raised a family on a kibbutz near the Sea of Galilee," Avra goes on, "never forgetting their roots from Spain to

France to this house. My mother, their only child, became Cindy's new special friend. She loved the doll and the frightening saga with my grandmother. The stories became an obsession with my mom—desperately wanting more details of her own childhood. Bubbe was very reluctant to discuss the horror but loved reminiscing about the good times here and the beauty of this home and land, which ironically provided comfort and luxury for elite German officers during the war. Mom always talked about coming back here to see where Grandma Rebecca grew up; she needed closure. My mother married her dream IDF soldier who tragically died in battle; it was a magnificent love affair. Unfortunately, Mom succumbed to cancer. I was just five years old with a baby sister, Becca, named after our grandmother. Because I was the oldest, Cindy was now mine.

"Every person in Israel, boy or girl, must serve the military, and I couldn't wait to help fulfill my destiny and make my grandparents and parents proud. So, I trained very hard and was lucky enough to be accepted into the Israeli Special Forces and ultimately the מסתערבים 'Mistaravim,' the counterterrorism group. Moishe and Zelig mentored me—with you and their plan in the background. They knew about this house I was able to repossess. Nazis kept great records, so it was easy to prove. It was my wish to Moishe that they use it in some form, to safeguard Israeli operatives.

"Well, the deal was done," Avra proclaims. "They would maintain it for me, reconfigure the infrastructure with ultra-modern and highly specialized cyber-stuff, and use it for special ops projects like this. In return, I would have an extraordinary country pied-a-terre to reconnect with my roots. My only stipulation was that they build a miniature mausoleum in honor of Bubbe, Mom, and Cindy so their spirits could finally return in peace and attain closure. Cindy is the guardian and keeper of their souls. She looks inward.

"Steven," staring at me with her intensely seductive brown eyes, "you and I have been followed very closely by the Israeli supra-government, an extremely secret paramilitary branch that 'doesn't exist.' The descendants of the founders of that black-ops office are sitting in this room. Just so you know, every detail and component of your participation in the extraction of the defector and your relationship with me, the facilitator, were planned by a select few in our respective militaries. It was no accident you were selected by your CO for this mission. It was a designed event," Avra declares.

"That Kassi bullshit in the restaurant was a set up to keep an eye on me?" I ask with astonishment.

"To protect you," she says. "The guy in the corner reading the newspaper is one of ours. He was monitoring Jabber when you killed him."

"Why is the Russian so fucking important?" I persist.

"The project is so highly sensitive and secure that only a few people are on a need-to-know basis," she explains, very seriously. "Suffice to say, he is a brilliant scientist. Secondly, the development of your double-agent status for the future is one of the most crucial intelligence operations our country has ever initiated. Millions of lives could be at stake; I will give you an extensive briefing tomorrow. Now is not the time—it is a moment of remembrance and celebration of life."

"This is bullshit. You're using me!" I rant.

Zelig interrupts and holds up his hand. "Quiet please, שקט בבקשה, shekat bevakasha, calm down—Steven. As time goes on, you will understand the significance of your life and awesome responsibilities. Enjoy the ride, my friend. Enough festivities for one night; everyone needs to get some sleep. We're leaving before dawn. The defector is having second thoughts... real nervous. Additionally, there's some serious chatter out there from the Russians. Eventually they'll figure it out. Gotta move soon and get our guy to a safe location in Cyprus. Steven's training will be real-time and maybe some live bullets—nothing like hot lead screaming by your head to develop a Mossad-op out of a boy scout."

"Cyprus?" I yell, "Thought they're advesarial to Israel?"

"That's what everyone thinks," Moishe explains. "Ha. Actually, they allow us to possess one of the best Israeli "inquiry labs" in the world—if you know what I mean—extremely valuable friend. We have a very understated but highly synergistic relationship with Cyprus, Greece, and Turkey and even the moderate Arab states— common enemies. Ya know the old saying, 'The enemy of my enemy is my friend.' Their strategic positions make them exceedingly important in the Eastern Mediterranean."

Zelig jumps in, "Can't allow the Americans to grab him first;

they'll never let go. Better if we get him secured—better for politics, better for everything. Must do it quietly though, stealth-like. In the long run, the possessor of exceptional knowledge usually perseveres. Luck is the variable, but intelligence and execution are a winning formula."

"Ok, everyone to bed," Avra interrupts. "Steven—get the air mattress from the closet: blow it up, or fuck it, or whatever—and sleep in that tiny guest room in the corner."

Chapter 46

Each night, when I go to sleep, I die. And the next morning, when I wake up, I am reborn.
— Mahatma Gandhi

Amid a much-needed deep sleep, albeit on a shitty mattress, all hell breaks loose; sounds like World War III is reverberating in the valley. There are explosions everywhere.

Jumping off the crummy floor futon where Avra banished me, I run into the hall. What the hell is going on? It's the middle of the night, but everyone is in full GO mode. I'm informed that there is major engagement in the valley. Intelligence spotted more of their SUVs.

Despite the horror, I can only focus on Avra's goddess-like body covered by a slinky T-shirt not really hiding her perky nipples. For one brief moment, I don't care what's happening except that she catches my stare and smiles... I know everything will be okay.

"Gotta get the defector now; they're on the move," Zelig yells. "This may be our last chance. Let's go, now. Hear me? Now, fucking now. Nowwwww!"

Avra, who had catapulted out of bed like being shot from a

cannon, refocuses her energy while getting her Uzi. On the other hand, I stand in the hallway with a massive hard-on. Go figure, I'm holding my dick, and Avra is prepping her Uzi for real action.

"You never hear the lightning that kills you," said Sister Shelley; she would be so proud. Could really use an ice-cold Schlitz. Was getting hard just thinking about that blessedly pure time when hard-ons were measured in hours, not inches. Everything was simple. People wore cotton and the Cleveland Indians were a force to be reckoned with. There were no terrorists that blew up babies.

"Mortars," Moishe yells as you could hear swishing sounds followed by huge explosions, one after another. "Everyone—do your job—meet at the designated coordinates. Can't let 'em get that Russian. Put your pants on, Steven, and let's get the fuck out of here," he orders.

It's astonishing how fast a boner retreats in a moment of crisis.

Lieutenant Roosh is escorted out the back door and told to fuck off. He will explain to his superiors that he fell, hit his head, and broke his mic. We will be in touch and send him copies of the pics so he can whack off to them. Real-life memories, ha! We own him.

According to the new intelligence, the defector's rendezvous point is about 10 miles from here. Zelig is barking instructions from the communication room and banging away at some keyboards.

Chapter 47

The explosions are getting louder and more intense. Grabbing Cindy and our weapons, Avra and I scoot out the back door, thrusting ourselves into what appears to be the second coming of *The War of The Worlds*. We hop into one of the specially-equipped off-roading, camouflage-colored Jeeps. They have massive Yokohama tires and air-driven MacPherson struts that can go anywhere—up the side of a mountain or through five feet of water. The undercarriage is totally waterproof. The only things that can stop us are bullets and trees.

"Ok. Roger. Out," Avra—speaking to her wrist.

Intelligence reports in real time... everything is fluid. A few more Iranian armored vehicles are detected and put out of their misery.

"Maybe they'll get the hint and back off for a while," she hisses. "On the other hand, it could attract negative scrutiny from the French. Fuck 'em."

I love when Avra gets her dander up, like a wildcat seeking a rat for dinner. Glad she's on my side.

Laser-guided rockets and their entrails pierce the foggy sky and illuminate the microscopic droplets creating a psychedelic effect. Amid the all-encompassing surround-sound, bombastic, earthquake-like permutations, a faint purring can be heard. At first, it's difficult to ascertain the source. Finally, it becomes apparent—there are fucking drones hovering above like birds-of-prey scoping out their next meal.

Without a doubt, some Howdy Doody Mossad cowboys who excel in everything, especially video games, are controlling these miniature flying fortresses from the comfort of an Air Force Base in the Negev desert.

From the stratosphere, a linear blast of vaporized viscera suffocates their targets in a millisecond of total incineration. Then, eerie black deadly calm—no sound, nothing—except the humming of the cute little drones heading home to sleep.

Avra catches my glance and winks. "Don't fuck with us!"

Chapter 48

All defectors have a complex relationship with
truth.
— David Mitchel, The Bone Clocks

The fog and smoke clear and reveal the most dazzling starlight I have ever seen. The Big Dipper—so vivid as if the finest champagne flows from her famous spout in honor of our ephemeral escape from tragedy. The near southwest foothills of the Pyrenees await our arrival; so does the defector.

Still in the Jeep fighting the ruggedness of the foothills; dawn has not yet appeared, so travel is safer than it will be in a few hours. Now, it's back to the camouflage of the world's best sanctuary—the omnipotent mountains where I left Jabber and met Avra, very apropos.

"What's so special about this Russian?" I vehemently ask Avra for the tenth time. "I know I'm an asshole who ran a 10.9-hundred-yard dash at Heights High and shed a slew of angry tacklers, but what fucking reason am I on a need-to-know basis?"

Avra tells me when a guy shows his 'roids, gets dominant, fired up, that's what turns her on. Well, I'm tired of sucking up to her, and

I tell her so. Screw that shit.

"There you go, Stevie boy," she says. "Got your balls a little ruffled, eh? Love it. Ha, so stunned with your ferociousness, gonna give you just a little inkling—a teensy weensy, little baby mother-fucking hint! You ready?"

"Yeah Avra, hit me with it…"

"Not sure if you can handle the facts," she says, coyly.

"Solid gold—very centered—I can handle anything," I tell her.

"How about XXXWMD?" she asks.

"What does that mean?" I wonder.

"Weapons of mass?" she prompts.

"Destruction?" finishing her sentence. "So, what is XXX?" I prod.

"Whaddaya think, Stevie?"

"Super X-rated," I answer.

"No, more than that," she responds.

"What the fuuuuuck, Avra? Ya mean BOOM?"

"I mean total annihilation!" she declares.

"For what—for whom?" I probe.

"For you Steven, your parents, kids, and all your friends."

"C'mon?" I say, with a little doubt.

"Everything—the whole fucking world—you, me and all the other motherfuckers." She responds with dread.

"Avra, whaddaya talking about? Don't exaggerate!" I plead.

"I'm a bad-ass bitch," she claims, "a secret Mossad black-ops fucking-killing machine who can slay you with my pinkie. I never exaggerate!"

"Oh my God—you're serious!" I gasp.

"BOOOOOOOOM. That's the hint, Steven—move on."

"So, you mean the defector is going to blow up something?" I ask, with trepidation.

"Not exactly," she replies.

"Ok... I need another hint," I say sternly.

"Yeah… BOOM. BOOM. BOOM. Bye-bye!" Avra raises her voice for emphasis.

"BOOM. BOOM. Bye-bye?" I probe.

"Yeah. bye-bye" she replies.

"Bye-bye what?" I ask desperately.

"The world!!" Avra blurts out like it's gonna happen in five minutes.

…silence…

…silence…

Chapter 49

THE ROXY

"Stop staring at me!" Avra scolds.

"Not staring, just stunned." I reply.

For some strange reason, I can't take my eyes off her deliciously delectable breasts. She definitely takes notice and just shakes her head, annoyed—like I'm a pervert or a fucking degenerate. Can't believe what she's saying, sounds like a science fiction movie— a horror film.

"No shit, Stevie. Listen," she explains, "our crucial mission is to secure this guy for Israel, nobody else, not even the U.S."

"Fuck. Jesus Christ, Avra, I'm an American soldier."

"Not really," she says. "Not exactly. Remember my little story about your life. Well, this is the payoff—your raison d'etre."

The only thing I can focus on is her exotic and tantalizing love-bush, her sacred Venus. Can taste it—smell it; driving me crazy as I fondly remember my excursion to the Roxy Burlesque in Cleveland when I was twelve years old...

———————

I didn't know the hole. I wasn't familiar with its construction. The terrain was foreign. I was perplexed, frightened, intimidated. What did the vagina look like? At that time, "Playboy" only had glimpses and airbrushed views. Guys would describe the mound of Venus as a valley of pleasure with flowers of passion and wet lips. When it was aroused, it was like a wet, hairy rain forest. Holy crap. Sounds great, but what did it really look like, and how did you communicate with it? None of my hotshot, cool pre-BAT brothers had really seen one. They saw glimpses and shadows, but only in the dark. Everybody talked about it. Guys heard from their older brothers, but not one of my friends had ever seen one in the flesh or even had a close encounter. I mean really seen one—talked to it, felt it, or made its owner moan. For sure, I was scared to death with anticipation. What was I going to do when we were finally introduced? Would I recognize it? How would I know if it was perfect or malformed? I had no idea what it looked like. I heard rumors and had seen sketches in hygiene class, but had never seen a picture. The Phys Ed teacher only discussed horrific stories about menstrual cycles and other insane events. Sounded awful, but I wanted one—a real one, needed it, deserved it. I was ready, but I didn't know what it looked like. How can I feel so passionate about something I've never seen or talked to? I was going crazy fantasizing about little hairy aliens between girl's thighs, creatures from outer space, man-eaters, Venus fly traps that killed you, or at the very least spread pestilence and disease.

How could I prepare for the great moment? The research was vague. Close encounters were not documented properly. I was being tormented until it suddenly came to me. A light went off. Wow! The Roxy Burlesque. Where else could a full-blown hormonal adolescent conduct original research than at the famous burlesque theater, the Roxy? Opened in 1931, the Roxy was the center for fun and sin on Cleveland's East side. Located on E. 9th Street and Chester, it was home to such famous strippers as Irma the Body, Blaze Starr, and Ann Curio, as well as comedians like Pinky Lee and Milton Berle. I wasn't interested in humor or silver buttons. I needed an anatomy lesson. The excitement was overwhelming. I could hardly keep it in my pants. So, at the age of 12, six months before my Bar Mitzvah, I made a man-type decision. I planned a trip to the Roxy.

It was a glorious Saturday in August, and I was going to the two o'clock matinee hopefully to finally set my eyes on a real vagina. Obviously, I wasn't able to drive yet, so I took the bus. Knowing the area pretty well because of previous trips to the Indians games, I felt very confident. It was an easy bus ride down Cedar Road. I asked a few of my friends to participate in the adventure but they were too nervous for whatever reason. Fine with me. Irma the Body was mine alone.

Saturday morning seemed like an eternity away. My mom kept asking me where I was going to spend the afternoon; I told her I was meeting my buddies at the Cedar-Lee Theater which was on the same bus line. At the time, we only had one car and my father had a meeting, so I would just take the bus. She gave me money for bus fare, snacks, and theater tickets. Little did she know that my matinee was hopefully with Irma's twat. High hopes. I had a big lunch, as my mother always insisted, and headed for the bus stop a block away.

The ride down Cedar Road was euphoric. Davis Bakery and Drexler's Pharmacy drifted by, and a block later Freddie's Poolroom passed on the right. Soon my future high school, Cleveland Heights, came into view, which was across the street from the Cedar-Lee Movie Theater where my mom knew I would be. It was surreal. People were getting on and off, but I was the only one going to the Roxy. The bus cruised past Coventry to Cedar Hill where you could see the great Terminal Tower that erupted from downtown like a throbbing penis. Very appropriate. The Heights: Cleveland, Shaker, and Mayfield were all elevated, and the views from this precipice were breathtaking, but I was more focused on my educational destination. Actually, I was beginning to study the "maftir" for my Bar Mitzvah, and my mom asked me if I practiced before I left. I told her, "Sure." Out of guilt, I brought the book with me so I could study on the bus. No way. I was too excited. There were times for studying your Haftorah, and there were times for studying the female anatomy. As we approached the East 9th Street stop, serious trepidation set in. It was a combination of excitement, guilt, and nerves. Really, where else would a twelve-year-old Jewish kid from Cleveland Heights want to be on a Saturday afternoon? I pulled on the stop cord, and it sounded like a fire alarm went off. Everyone, or so I thought, turned around and stared at me. I was so embarrassed because, surely, they all knew where I was going. I had to get off immediately. After an eternity, the bus finally stopped. I made my way to the front carrying my stuff: the Haftorah book, my bus fare, and my snacks neatly packed into a small, brown paper bag. Very clever. Everyone probably wondered why I was getting off in front of the burlesque theater. I am sure my face was bright red as I stepped into the exit well.

Why wasn't the door opening? Please hurry. I've got to get off.

Finally, the bus door creaked open. I stepped down onto the curb and looked up. There she was in all her glory, Irma the Body, thirty feet high and looking right at me. I knew I came to the right place. She was captivating and seemed to be calling out to me and saying, "I'm glad you came."

Irma—you don't know the half of it. I wanted her. I needed her to teach me.

Everyone in downtown Cleveland appeared to be watching. I pulled the brim of my Chief Wahoo hat over my face so no one would recognize me. I kept my head down trying to assimilate into the throng of humanity. Impossible. It seemed like thousands of people were focused on my arrival. A little paranoia, perhaps. Total excitement, for sure. I felt like everyone was screaming, "look at that kid going to the strip joint! Look at him! Look at him!"

I thought I would throw up. I was shaking. My very own first vagina was just on the other side of the ticket booth. It was only 100 feet away, but it could've been a mile. Each step felt like my feet were stuck in concrete. I had to get out of the crowd, although the show wasn't starting for an hour and the doors didn't open for thirty minutes. What was I going to do? I needed to get inside. The only one stopping me was this mean-looking old man at the ticket window with a fat cigar and a big brown wide-brimmed fedora covering half his face. There was a big sign above the window saying, "No one under 18 admitted."

He snarled, "Whaddaya want, kid?"

I whispered, "A ticket."

"Can't you see da sign?" he barked.

"Yes sir," I answered, timidly.

"A buck," he snarled back.

"It's only twenty-five cents," I pleaded.

"A buck," he grumbled.

"Ok," finally relenting. I would have paid anything.

With great trepidation and hormonal delight, I gave the guy a buck and walked in. If he only knew that I would have given him my last penny to experience what I was breathlessly anticipating. Soon, my life would never be the same... I hoped. Entering the pavilion was exhilarating. Red-flocked wallpaper caressed the magnificent parlor adorned by crystal chandeliers and intricate woodcarvings. I had never seen anything like it in my young life. Although the golden age of burlesque was dying, remnants such as the Roxy were still alive.

"Thank you, Lord!" I moaned.

An hour to kick off. How would I survive the anticipation? I was so proud of myself for having the determination and creativity to not only plan this wonderful adventure, but to actually carry it out. Today, I will become a man. Excuse me, Mister Bar Mitzvah. Reconnoitering my surroundings and realizing I was the first to arrive, I decided to take a leak. In those days pissing was a nonissue and took about fifteen seconds. Today, taking a wiz is an art form. Arriving at the urinal, I pulled the zipper down and out popped my guy raring to go. He wasn't sure if he was supposed to pee or check out Irma, although he was pretty, pretty, pretty excited. For those of you not in the know, it's very difficult to pee with a hard-on. Somehow, I persevered.

Watching the clock was like observing a plant grow. I was a tender shoot; impatient for growing season, eager to bloom.

Maybe I should find a seat, I said to myself, or anybody who was listening.

The ticket taker, a disgusting, fat, hairy lady doubling as the popcorn-maker greeted me. Great idea. Buy some popcorn and find a seat. "Whaddaya vandt?" she grunted.

"Small popcorn, please," I said.

"Are you blind?" she scolded. "We only have one fucking size."

"Okay, and a small cherry coke."

"Are you stupid, too?" she replied with even more disdain. "We only have one fucking size."

Wow, I thought. She was meaner than that asshole outside.

This better be worth it. I gave my ticket to the carnival queen and entered the theater.

"Holy shit!" I said out loud.

The old venue was luxurious but much smaller than I imagined. Very intimate. Perfect for my needs. Obviously, I had to be in the front row to see details. No problem. It was still empty, and I had my choice. The stage was slightly elevated, and I would be able to look right up her crack and even reach out and touch it. My dreams would come true. I picked a seat right in the middle of the row. The situation could not have been better. Only a half-hour to go as I slowly started to eat my popcorn and study my Maftir. My mom would be proud.

I could hear other patrons entering from behind and feel their strange glances. I focused on the curtain, imagining what was going to be unveiled. Sensing a throng of people taking their seats, I hesitated to turn around in case someone would recognize me. Although highly unlikely, you never know. Anything could happen. My Sunday school teacher, Mr. Rubin, was arrested for robbing a bank. What a dumbass! Anyway, you can never be too careful. Sensing the seats filling up around me, I stuck my face in the Haftorah book and lowered the brim of my Cleveland Indians hat while chowing down on the popcorn, desperately seeking Nirvana.

Without warning, the lights started to blink. Not knowing what was occurring, and against my better judgment, I turned around, imagining the worst, like a police raid for underage patrons. My heart was racing; I was sweating profusely. Soon I realized the flickering was really a call for action. Showtime. The patrons became real. The hall was incredibly packed. Wow. Regular-looking people; a lot of guys, but shockingly also some good-looking ladies. Maybe they were stripper wannabes. They were probably just here for a good time or maybe an education, just like me. Suddenly, I felt a deep kinship for my fellow burlesque attendees. Imagine, years from now, I would look back and share this moment in time with these wonderful folks. Maybe even a reunion.

Suddenly the lights went out, and the orchestra started playing "Yankee Doodle Dandy." The curtain rose to a thunderous applause. This was it. My fantasy. My very first vagina. Incredibly—instead of Irma, out came this little bald-headed guy jumping up and down.

"What's going on? Where's Irma?" I said out loud.

I guess the guy next to me heard and laughed. "Don't worry, kid. She'll be here; the last act, but she's worth it!"

"You mean, I have to wait till the end?" I asked.

"Yeah kid, but these comedians are really funny," he said, with authority. "Sit back, relax, and enjoy the show."

As it turned out, the first act was hysterical. Despite my nervous excitement, I could laugh with the rest of the folks. My seat-mate was this nice, gentle, bifocaled old man about my grandfather's age who explained that burlesque was just as much about comedy as stripping. That may have been true, but I wasn't there for the laughs— just serious education. When in Rome, though...

The jokes came fast and furious; one ugly-looking comedian after another and all very funny. Burlesque, as I've been told, was the beginning of some other very famous show people such as Red Buttons, Phil Silvers, and Abbott and Costello: "Who's on first?"

An hour passed, and I still had not seen a vagina; not only that, now it was intermission. Everybody got up, peed, smoked, and bought popcorn. I was getting very anxious and needed the real deal. The seductive mound of Venus was waiting for me. The break was very nerve-racking. I had to pee but didn't want to show my face or my penis.

For crying out loud, I just got hair on my balls!

It seemed like everyone was screaming, "What's that perverted kid doing at a burlesque show on a Saturday afternoon in the summertime? He should be out playing baseball."

Maybe they were right, but I was on a mission. I needed to see it, to smell it, and become intimately acquainted. I could no longer just leave it up to my imagination or rely on stories from my friends' older brothers. It was driving me crazy. I needed one of my own, but before that I had to do my homework, like studying the Talmud whose laws would guide me to the Promised Land and purification. I was getting close; ten feet to be exact and two minutes to the second half.

The lights started to flicker, and my heart rate accelerated into outer space. Showtime! Hysterical, giddy, frightened, and aroused. That pretty well sums it up. I've waited my whole life for this—the moment that would change me forever. I could hardly think. Everyone in the audience must've been staring at me. Hey, they're all here, too.

What's their excuse? I was here strictly for a scholastic encounter, researching from source material—the purest way to learn.

Oh my God, the curtains were rising—evidence close at hand indicated I was, too. "Ladies and gentlemen: direct from Las Vegas— the sultry, sexy vixen with a little red wagon—none other than the tantalizing, erotic Miss Patti Waggin."

"Who?" I screamed. "Who is she? Where is Irma? Where is Irma the Body?"

"Don't worry, kid," the guy next to me said. "The Body is coming."

Patti was pretty cute. She pulled a little red American Flyer' wagon in sexy, saucy ways I'd never seen. That wagon was her byline and her main prop. She did everything on the wagon a woman could do. She stood on it confidently, tits and hips screaming "I dare you"; she sat on it, submitting, timid and inviting at once. She even did handstands, rousing the audience—at least me—with bonus action as she walked on her hands with perfect rhythm around that red wagon. Finally, she made strutting a fine art as she pulled her teddy bear around the stage, teasing those of us close enough to pick up on delicious innuendo.

'Boom da da boom da da boom.' Finally, she began to strip. She had come out in red overalls with pink feathers in a giant hat. Everything started coming off very slowly. I was going crazy. Maybe she would be the one to solve my problems. The hat was gone. The feathers were next.

'Boom da da boom da da boom.' Carefully and agonizingly deliberate, she unbuttoned her overall straps. First the left, then the right. The pants were next; she coaxed them down ever so slowly, revealing her voluptuous hips.

'Boom da da boom da da boom.'

She was wearing a matching red brassiere and panties. I had only seen my mother's—and they weren't red... I was delirious with anticipation. This could be it.

'Boom da da boom da da boom.' Patti sat in her wagon in her confident mode: chest out, hands pressing the wagon floor, legs open in invitation. One hand now sliding upward, then the other. Off came the brassiere. I had hoped to see all of her lusciousness, but red stars on her nipples thwarted my dreams. Standing slowly, she brought art to taking panties down her wondrous thighs.

What the fuck? There was a pink feather covering her vagina.

Please, God. Let it happen.

She held out her hands asking the crowd, "More?"

Everyone stood and cheered in unison, "Take it off!"

'Boom da da boom da da boom.' Off came the stars. They were the most tantalizing, pink, ripe nipples I had ever seen. Again, only my mom's and, oh—that's right—my next-door neighbor's. But the fact is I didn't make this odyssey to E. 9th Street just to see nipples. We were getting agonizingly close to the holiest of holies, the Gadol of imagination, and the field of dreams.

'Boom da da boom da da boom.' Standing in her wagon, with

her nipples staring at me with deep understanding and passion, Miss Patti yanked away the pink plume protecting her garden of Eden.

"No, no," I whispered. There was a tiny patch covering my dream.

"What is that?" I said out loud, louder than I thought.

"It's a G-string," my new friend said.

Again, Patti raised her hands, cupped her breasts, and the crowd cheered. I could see the faint edges of my obsession, the glorious pubic hairs trying to escape from their barrier. I was so close and yet so far. I could smell it. Patti raced off the stage to a standing ovation. I needed more. This wouldn't do. Internal frenzy.

My friend put his arm around me and said, "That's all. It's against the law to show more."

I was dumbfounded. Getting a girlfriend was my only solution. My anticipation and obsession with Irma were anti-climactic. I already knew the outcome. Deep frustration. Agony.

"Where was the ecstasy?" I whispered.

As it turned out, "The Body" was a huge disappointment—not because she didn't bare all, but she was a fat, over-the-hill, disgusting lady whose real name was Mary Goodneighbor. She wasn't my choice for a good neighbor ... Bring back Patti! Mary Goodneighbor should have stayed backstage—or in her own neighborhood. Very apropos. I am sure in her day she was spectacular, but not on this Saturday afternoon six months before my Bar Mitzvah. Like OJ, she didn't know when to quit.

It was an excellent adventure that I will never forget. I didn't make it to the summit, but not because I didn't try. I didn't arrive at the Promised Land, but not because I didn't dream. What a great day! I learned I could accomplish anything. I just needed a girlfriend.

"Hi, mom. I'm home. What's for dinner?"

Chapter 50

We take the Jeep as far as it can take us. The abandoned trails are way too narrow, so we hide it in a tall grass field and mark the location. We will have to trek and climb during the rest of our yet-unknown journey, awaiting further intelligence.

As the first hint of light appears over the horizon, I suddenly have a terrific urge to piss, really bad. Shuffling behind the nearest bush, ready to donate a bucket of urine to the local environment, I whip it out—but no dice.

"Hurry the fuck up!" she prods.

Trying—it ain't happening—not so easy when you absolutely have to piss, but you can't. Trying to concentrate… focus, c'mon, man… focus. She has no idea… girls don't have prostates.

Flashback to a freezing winter day in the old Cleveland Municipal Stadium. The Browns were playing the Baltimore Colts, and the temperature was zero with a wind-chill of -10. Brrrr. I had to piss so bad at halftime that I ran to the bathroom and almost peed in my pants. But sure enough, when I got there and unleashed my cock from under three layers of clothing, the damn thing wouldn't work. Everybody was crowding in and forming lines twenty deep and guys were yelling in unison, "Hurry the fuck up! ... piss...piss...piss!"

"Steven, put your hose away… let's go!" Avra yells.

"Almost done. Avra, don't you ever have to pee?"

"No, not human; don't even fart," she says, matter-of-factly.

Finally, dawn is breaking. We hike up the mountain to the nearest ledge which allows a 180° view of the magnificent plain below.

"Roger. Fuuuuuuck... fuuuuuuuck… fuuuuuuuuuck!!!" Avra screams as her gizmo vibrates.

"What happened? What?" I ask, with deep concern.

Silence.

More silence.

It's bad news. We've lost contact with the op-agent immediately responsible for the defector's hand-off. The last known position, about an hour ago, was five kilometers from here. They're unresponsive to any communication. Working blind, we don't even know if they're captured or dead.

"This is a clusterfuck," she yells. "We have to find him, now. Critical. Whoever acquires this information will control the world— or destroy it! Do you understand me, Steven? Do you? Do you fucking understand?"

"No, I don't. You said I was on a need-to-know. What are you talking about? Tell me—tell me now. Avra, what the hell is going on?"

Chapter 51

COLONIC

Me: Yes, I'd like some colon cleanse. It's
something that cleans you out, so your
antidepressants work better.
Pharmacist: I think you're using your
antidepressants wrong. They go in your mouth.
— Jenny Lawson

Never seen Avra like this: terrified, anxious, losing control, and she won't tell me why.

"Ya know—it'll make you feel better—like a colon cleansing, a purge or even a vomit," I point out.

"I'm good... really," she assures me, although I don't believe her. "I certainly don't need my colon cleansed—it's perfect—too bad you'll never get near enough to know." Avra becomes strangely silent for two to three minutes—sort of lost in space and time. Suddenly she whispers, "Miniaturization."

"What? What are you talking about?" I am clueless.

Avra proceeds to finally disclose the importance of the mission—the discovery of the long sought-after ability to miniaturize nuclear weapons. It's the dramatic unearthing of the sacred code of the atomic age. The defector theorized that by combining reverse-3D-modeling formulas with highly specialized nanoparticles, he could construct a micro sub-atomic bomb. It is the basis of the creation of the universe—like a black hole, only micro. This is what every scientist through the ages predicted was possible, but nobody proved it except for Holtzmann Viktor, our precious defector.

Israeli intelligence has been after him for years. The man is a genius, I am told, a mad scientist—a rogue Russian. They were even afraid of him. He has no living family—nothing frightens him—he can't be bought or threatened. The good news is he hates the Russians and was very receptive to our agents pulling him out.

During the Stalin regime, his family was killed in the Ukraine. Holtzmann's parents were considered enemies of the state and disappeared with millions of other poor souls. Viktor, a scientific prodigy, was pardoned from this horrible demise because of his extreme brilliance. The government educated him with the finest tutors in the land and nurtured him to be the mastermind of their new top-secret futuristic atomic research lab, but he had other ideas.

For unexplained reasons, all his educators and mentors somehow disappeared—totally eradicated. 'There is no such thing as a coincidence,' as they say in the spiritual world.

Avra continues to brief me with more details, praying that

somehow our intel will be restored. Hopefully, they're stuck in another cave and unable to communicate for the time being. No other scenario is good. The tension is thick enough to knife through. Avra is so upset that she ducks behind a tree and pukes. I can hear her retching.

She reappears, wiping her mouth.

"Sorry about that, Steven. It would be a fucking nightmare if we lost Viktor and the handler—my baby sister, Becca."

"The handler is your sister? Wow, shit!" I say, astonished. "No wonder you've been so upset; that explains everything. Don't worry— we'll find them, I know we will. We have to!"

After regaining her composure, she resumes the briefing and continues to spill her guts out. The guy, it turns out, is the second coming of Einstein, only smarter, and he has the luxury of using modern supercomputers with their awesome processing power. Imagine what Albert could have done with just an Apple IIe or... the latest governmental, quantum rip-ass motherfuckin' supercomputers.

Concurrently, every theoretical nuclear physicist was trying to miniaturize reactions for increased power and deliverability—but nobody could produce the ultimate fusion—create a minuscule black hole—a real black fucking hole—until now. Secretly, he was able to super-compress the particles into zero mass and then decompress the mass vacuum to create immense energy... the likes of which humanoids have never seen.

Interestingly, Viktor was a loner, very peculiar indeed. He was so incredibly brilliant and demanding that they gave him carte-blanche. The government built him a super-secret research facility in Kasimov, a small town on the bank of the Oka River, well known for its cheap, crappy vodka, but not its futuristic nuclear site. What it did have was an endless water supply to mitigate the intense heat produced by the facility's byproducts. The covert clandestine state monitored his work and required monthly reports of current data and research, but he was so cantankerously quirky, they basically left him alone. On the surface, he had a team of 300 quantum and particle physicists working for him. What they didn't know—Viktor was privately fabricating false and misleading data with distorted and deceptive assumptions that were deliberately generated for the government's eyes.

He had secretly discovered an age-old dream of scientists—the Holy Grail of theoretical physics—artificially recreating a black hole. He developed the ability to produce ultra-micro nano-particle fusion reactions that were sub-atomic bombs—smaller than a quark or lepton but 100,000 times stronger than Hiroshima.

For the first time, I understand why the intelligence concerning Viktor is so shocking. Imagine what a villain could do with the undetectable ability to deliver the product in any imaginable way: vapor, gas, satellite, high energy lasers, or even by hand for the ultimate suicide bomb. The world would never be the same!

"Steven, this is your need-to-know time," Avra explains. "Maybe you can help save the world. In this case, the present is not the present—the gift is the future to preserve for our children."

Chapter 52

As we trek up the mountain, waiting and hoping for updates on Viktor's location, my immediate focus is on her butt just a few feet in front of me. So close and yet so far.

"I have eyes behind my head. Are you listening to me or just staring at my ass?" she asks.

"Both. I'm very good at multitasking. Do you really want to quiz me, Avra? For sure I know exactly where your butt crack starts."

"You're so annoying, Steven," she answers.

The main hiking trail is far too crowded, so we use an old accessory path that nobody knows about. It's very overgrown, but perfect for our immediate needs.

During our journey, Avra explains that the Russian is the maven of future nuclear physics—the Gadol—the most brilliant quantum fusionist in the world. He *could* be the harbinger of peace, energy, and medicine. Instead he just wants retribution—to destroy Russia. So, he dedicated his life to memorializing his parents, grandparents, brothers, and sisters. Viktor swore an oath to their memories, to do away with the Russians and their rulers. It's surprising what you can learn on a hiking trail in the Pyrenees. He is a real sociopath—for good reason. They broke his heart.

With tears welling up, Avra tells me, "The Mossad had their eye on Holtzmann for twenty years and had a plan to get him home, and now—look at this horrible fuck-up."

"Don't be so hard-on yourself; it's not your fault," I plead.

"Yes, it is. The whole plan was my idea. Shit. I sold a lot of people on the strategy. I went all in. My baby sister is in dire straits. Can't believe it's going down the toilet. We're so close. Please let it happen!"

Avra explains that, early on, they recognized his remarkable intelligence and once-in-a-millennium potential. He has Jewish heritage but obviously was never allowed to practice his religion. So, the only way to turn him was through his heart. Coincidentally, ten years ago, he met a sensuous, young Russian pianist who just happened to be a planted Mossad agent. She blurts out, "Ha, remember, there's no such thing as a coincidence. Her name is Becca, my sister, a shayna maidela—Yiddish for a beautiful Jewish girl, and, by the way—a phenomenal soldier. She is his handler, but now she's gone."

She paused, wiped her nose.

"Fuuuuuuck!" Avra screams as loud as she can.

Wow, I've never seen her like this. There's gotta be something more she's not telling me. Her heart's exploding. Don't know what to say anymore—everything is so fucked up—unreal. My life is a charade. Difficult to grasp—just a Jewish kid from Cleveland Heights.

We are silent for a while, listening to the wispy breeze rushing through the woods of cypress without a care in the world. Life will go on for the wind and the trees and the rest of nature, but maybe not for Becca.

Dawn is breaking; it's a beautiful morn. The sky, a bright blue; the air, crisp—allowing nature's dew to rejuvenate the thirsty foliage and elicit the therapeutic jasmine aroma. How do I know condensation increases as the dew point decreases? Well, after taking that memorable summer physics class, I became an expert, but that's a whole different story.

In the meantime Avra and I hike up the mountain, trying to enjoy the magnificent plain below with the River L'Ariège meandering through the foothills of the great Pyrenees, proudly reflecting the steadfast rising sun. You can see forever but it's difficult to focus not knowing Becca's status.

Off to the side are the incredible remnants of an ancient cave which has been fortified over the years with an array of huge multi-colored stones, seemingly decorated by our creator with intermingling verdant grass, moss, and ferns.

What a glorious day this will be, I think, as the mist is climbing from the valley and the sunshine begins to bathe the lush vegetation with its warmth. Embracing our mystical surroundings, however, would be pathetically futile. We're on a critical mission to save humanity from a horrifying weapon of mass destruction. Time is running out for Becca, the defector, and the world. There are only a few more grains of sand left in our hourglass.

Chapter 53

Time has come today
— Chambers Brothers

Our gizmos break the stillness like a bolt of lightning when you least expect it.

"Roger that. Oooooooooh!" She screams.

"What? What happened?" I plead. "Tell me."

"Oh, thank God, Steven. She left the cave and is on the move." Avra yells. "She's ok. Alive. Oh God, thank you!" She starts sobbing. "Thank you, God," as she grabs me, crying on my shoulder. It feels so good as I wrap her in my arms and let her cry. She thanks me for my support and understanding.

"Head out now," she orders our team. "C'mon, Steven—this is your time to shine, motherfucker—your moment of glory. Let's bring Becca home."

Turning to the magnificent, ancient cave—what a perfect place to piss.

"Hurry the fuck up," Avra orders.

Girls don't understand that peeing is an art form—but relieving myself in this majestic setting is spiritual. Trying to rush just makes it more difficult.

I hear footsteps as I shake off the last drop and turn to see two frickin' terrorists aiming AK-47s at Avra's head.

"Look here," I say, pointing to my dick, as I shoot 'em between the eyes. They stare in disbelief.

"Li-li-lick that, you muuuuutherfuckers." Ha, just as I was taught.

"Oh my God—that's the greatest thing I've ever seen!" Avra yells.

"Which? My cock or my Glock?"

"Both… yikes… saved my life… you're my hero. Where did you learn to shoot like that?" she asks incredulously.

"Ya know… Army Ranger training is pretty good," I proudly declare.

"Holy shit! You can say that again," she says jokingly.

"Okay I will. Army Ranger training is..."

"Just kidding—shut the fuck up and put your cock away... before I get too horny," she tells me with a little smirk. "Seriously, that was a mighty quick reaction for a rookie. Hmm."

"You can say that again," I reply, with a shit-eating grin.

"Ha, Stevie—just got excited because I wasn't killed. Ya know... if you had missed—we'd both be dead."

"Yea, but you would've always thought I was a wimp," I tell her.

"Well—you're not a wimp," as she grabs my bicep. "Nice iron.

C'mon, let's go before some more assholes find us."

"Wait—gotta put my tools away," I say, proudly.

Avra just shakes her head and grins.

"My hero, let me give you a big hug," as she puts her arms around me.

"Wow, all this for shooting two assholes?" I ask, feeling a boner emerging.

"Steven," comes a whisper in my ear. "On the count of three, drop to the ground immediately. Understand?"

"Yeah."

"One, two, three," she murmurs slowly.

In one magic moment, like a choreographed dance, I crumple as Avra whips out her Beretta and whacks two more shitheads hiding in a tree.

"Whoa, you are something. Fuckin' great shooting... You're almost as good as me. Now... you saved my life," I bellow.

"Better than you," she says.

"No, you're not," I brag, grabbing her left arm and flipping her in the air with my new Krav Maga move.

"Whoa, buster," kicking me in the balls, as she reverse-pivots, comes around and gets me in a choke-hold.

"OOOOOOH… my nuts…. OOOOOOOOOH!" I yelp, gasping for air but I manage to reverse her again, cutting her legs out.

"They don't know Krav Maga like we do—Israel Defense Forces perfected it," she says proudly, bending my left wrist, almost breaking it.

"AHHH. Ok, ok, you made your point. Now what am I gonna do with my hard-on and sore balls?" I quiz her.

Avra just snickers, saying, "Hang on cowboy, pace yourself—first gotta find Becca, now that we know she's ok."

Chapter 54

They are mobile, about two miles from here—intel informs us we have an hour to intercept before it's too late. The crazy fucking Iranian terrorists, whose brains we just splattered over the poppy field, have other brothers who are coming hard—the A team.

The long intel message notes there is an abundance of Russian chatter. Even though they finance these assholes, they don't want the Iranians to get him. That would give Zeman too much leverage. They're really pissed off and embarrassed that Viktor defected. It's going to be interesting. Our top priority is to secure his micro hard drive and, of course, Becca.

From his resume, even without the black hole discovery, Viktor is still the most prominent theoretical nuclear physicist in the world. He would be a major coup for any country or terrorist organization seeking to establish nuclear supremacy. The black hole is the icing on the cake. The balance of world power depends on it. Nobody knows about the miniaturization discoveries except a special few in Israel. It would be like winning the Powerball—an apocalyptical jackpot if someone else were to obtain this information.

The fundamentalist jihadist terrorists are the most frightening because they would deploy the weaponry immediately. It would be the end of Israel for sure—and maybe the entire free world. They are ultra-fanatical fundamentalists who would be willing to die for the destruction of the Zionist State and her allies, including the moderate Sunni Arab countries: Jordan, Egypt, and Saudi Arabia. Armageddon is real—failure is not an option. This is probably the most critical mission for the future of Israel.

Becca has amazingly reestablished communication with the rest of the unit, employing a special inter-synchronized scrambled logarithm that's transparent only to her handlers somewhere in Israel, then relayed to us.

Raffi, Moishe, and Zelig, approaching from the westerly flank, are closer to the newly designated extraction point. Avra and I are heading to point zero from the east.

"Lots of shit going down, Avra; not what I expected on my first assignment."

"Steven," she scolds, "are you starting up with that crap again? This is crunch time baby—seventh game, World Series: two outs, bottom of the ninth, down by one—and you're batting. Can you get it up? Can you, motherfucker? Get your head on straight, asshole."

Staring at her tits—wanting her more than anything—I scream deep from my innards, "Let's fucking do it! Bring Becca home."

Chapter 55

Explosions are booming everywhere. Holy shit—there's nothing like real live fire to get your blood flowing, and that's not a metaphor, but you still die. The ferocious Iranian terrorists are indiscriminately shooting at anything that moves. They will say they were protecting their diplomats, which of course is bullshit. Mortars, RPGs, and snipers are howling. The combination of smoke and fog gives the foothills a rather mystical quality. Cindy, in my backpack, starts to tremble—poor thing.

Incredibly, we are not dead. Mr. Garf Zeman and his fucking fanatics start shooting indiscriminately like the Wild West. It's *Gunsmoke* all over again; Avra is Kitty, and I am Marshall Matt Dillon, but more like Festus the fuck-up, but who cares? Just get us outta here in one piece.

"These fuckers obviously don't know the location of Becca and Holtzmann, or else they would've had 'em by now," Avra says, hopefully.

She's right. They're just attempting to generate chaos and movement. According to our former prisoner, First Lieutenant Roosh, there was a Russian mole who leaked Holtzmann's disappearance to the Iranians, obviously for a rather large sum of money. People do the wildest things. He also corroborated the presence of Zeman, who would do anything to snatch Viktor. The crazy Islamic terrorists are the worst kind of adversaries—not afraid to die.

Through the sound of the explosions, we can hear the humming of drones overhead like eagles looking for their breakfast. Cindy becomes very peaceful, and her trembling stops as if she knows something.

Our birds of prey light up the sky like New Year's Eve at midnight. It's a thousand-year solar flare storm. Nothing remains— NO THING—not even pieces to send home to their mothers. "Holy moly," Cindy says, smiling.

It's not like a football game where each side cheers when their team scores. We are just trying to stay alive and bring our people home. Nevertheless, it's a spectacular pyrotechnic show, and our team just had a big pass play.

"Wow, Avra, this is like when we rescued Cindy from the mausoleum—full out conflagration—so frickin' cool," I declare.

"No shit, Sherlock," she says. "Same amazing video gamers. They love it, but unlike all the other geeks who blowup animations— these fuckers could kill with their eyes closed—for real."

To be a drone-gamer, they first have to qualify in the field and be real-time battle tested warriors, very special motherfuckers. They have done it all: blown heads off, drawn blood, and dismantled bombs. It's a lot harder killing people when you don't see their faces—terrible nightmares.

"By the way, Avra, I really enjoyed shooting those fuckers when I was peeing… very invigorating." She just laughs.

Bottom line, it was a major fuck-up that they got so close. We still don't know how it happened but will find out soon enough when we review the game tape Monday morning like the NFL does. Everybody is graded. Procedures are analyzed, and analytics are synthesized. That's how you get better. We can't afford screw ups—lucky this time—next time, maybe not so fortunate. These assholes can be lucky just once. We must be right every time.

"Let's get Becca home, Steven—she's been gone way too long. Can't wait for you to meet her," Avra says with a big grin.

Can hear Cindy in the backpack saying, "Oh boy."

Chapter 56

Hello, Dolly!
— Jerry Herman

"We have eyes on her. There's Becca—oh my God!" Avra screams with pure joy. Raffi, so excited he can hardly talk, tears welling up in his solemn eyes—eyes that have seen it all, good and bad.

The thistle separates as a gentle breeze comforts all the valley's inhabitants. Emerging from nature's womb, Becca appears. Avra runs up and hugs her baby sister as they both cry. So pure. Such a heartwarming reunion, goosebumps overwhelm me. The wind ceases, the leaves go still, and no one breathes.

All I can muster is, "Hello, Dolly."

"Hey," she says, with a smile that sucks me in.

Stunned…. "Hey," I repeat softly.

"Hey, yourself," she offers back.

"What the fuck?" Avra shrieks.

Paralyzed—never in my life have I ever visualized such a delicious image—except for Avra, of course. Becca brushes off the foliage from her radiant jet-black tresses as she sweeps her hands over her delectable breasts and hips.

"Holy shit, here we go again," Cindy murmurs as she rolls her eyeless eyes.

Becca's body is dreamlike, with astonishingly long legs that come together in such harmony, creating a delta of ecstasy that I could die for—just 30 seconds to peek under her panties. That's all I ask, remembering my glorious day in search of Irma the Body's Venus at the Roxy Burlesque.

That's only the beginning—her face could light a million stars with large sparkling brown eyes that emerge over elegant cheekbones. The shimmering black hair tapers just over her freckled shoulders and a tight low-cut tank top accentuates her scrumptiously succulent nipples. Getting such a freaking hard-on; can't walk or speak, so I just gawk.

Avra glares at me. "Don't even think about it—don't you dare, you pervert—she's my little sister, for God's sake. Why don't you go behind that tree and jerk off or get some ice water on that freaking baseball bat of yours. You are so fucked up! If you ever look at her again like that, I'll throw you over the cliff."

Some little sister! That explains everything. Oh my God, yikes—well, there's definitely a strong resemblance. I wish I could see their mother. Oh man, she must've been something, remembering the old adage of first checking out the mother of a prospective new girlfriend. Can't keep my eyes off her thighs; they are perfect. In terms of chicken thighs, my grandmother always told me, in no uncertain terms, to check out the mother hen.

With delight, I relive a beautiful memory from my childhood:

———————

THE CHICKEN MAN

The maturation of the olfactory senses and subsequent appreciation for the sexual bouquet given off by the female body doesn't happen overnight. It takes years of training. My development began with the chicken man. The events that I shall recount are so vividly ingrained in my memory that it's startling. At the age of four, my mother and grandmother would take me to the kosher chicken store on Taylor Road in Cleveland Heights. It was a small facility with a bunch of live chickens and a "shochet." He is a person, a pious man, who has had special training and certification in the laws of "shechita" or the kosher preparation of food. A chicken must be handled and slaughtered correctly to maintain its kosher status. The most important aspect, however, is to select the proper chicken. The criteria are simple: smell, feel, and instinct. My grandmother, as taught by her grandmother, learned what the supreme essence should be. The poignant fragrance must be perfect. It can't be described. It must be experienced. You'll know it when you know it. She physically lifted each chicken, spread their thighs, and gave a whiff. It had to be just right: the ideal fragrance, the absolute essence, and the once-in-a-lifetime chicken.

I'm not kosher, but my grandmother would be very proud. On that memorable spring morning of 1950, I began the lifelong process of selecting the ultimate woman. My Bubbe had me check out each hen and instructed me with hands-on experience. I was a quick learner and looked forward to our visits at the chicken store. Soon I was able to pick out the best chicken by smell, although my Bubbe had to give the final approval. She was convinced that this was the beginning process of picking a lifetime mate. It wasn't just about the proper essence between the legs; it was tactile feedback of the "pulkes" (Yiddish for thighs)—not too skinny and not too fat. After all, you would not want to get lost in an abyss of 'schmaltz.' There has been some anecdotal evidence that schmaltz turns into cellulite. When you probe the thighs of a young chicken, make sure that the pulkes don't take finger imprints. My Bubbe stressed that the pulkes should not be fully developed at an early age. As a matter of fact, being too skinny at a young age is better than being too schmaltzy. It is better to err on the lean side. Skinny thighs can always develop, but schmaltzy legs will only get schmaltzier later in life. Another Bubbe-ism is to make sure you check out the mother hen. Even though a cute little chick with lean pulkes looks okay now, you must initiate your due diligence. Proper examination of the mature hen will portend the future. If the hen is a 'milf'—a mother I'd like to fuck—there's a good chance that the immature chick is a 'milf' in the making. If, on the other hand, a robust young fowl with a super stout mother hen presents herself, run as fast as you can to the chicken store down the street. Most young roosters like well-developed pulkes at an early age, but their focus is short term. They want immediate gratification. That's okay, but you must be consistent in your rationale. You don't want to be smothered in a bed of thick schmaltzy thighs or a sea of cellulite at the age of 50 when you have ignored all the telltale signs at the age of 14. Thighs, schmaltz, whiff or sniff—it was more about the guttural interpretation of the character of the chicken—a look in their eyes, a yearning in their heart, and a peering into their soul. It has much to do with moral fiber and zealous passion. You have to ask the question, "Does this chicken have what it takes, or does it want to be chicken soup and spam? More importantly does this chick just want to get laid or does she have that special passion for the long haul?"

Hopefully, life lessons are learned at every turn—the path you take; the fork in the road; the choices you make. It is astonishing, at the age of four with your Bubbe at a kosher chicken store, that buying a chicken becomes a life-altering event. Each day is an archaeological tell in the layers of life. My grandmother was very proud and knew as I got older my early lessons with her and the "shochet" would forever prove invaluable. The accumulation of experiences promotes the ability to make future decisions. Your actions are predicated upon previous choices and responses. Every essence, sensory or intellectual, is derived from genetic and learned behavior. The ratio varies just like chicken soup, a pinch of this and a 'bissel,' (Yiddish for little) of that. It cures all ills!

With a warm feeling in my heart after reliving the special days with my grandmother, I introduce myself, just to be friendly. "Hello Dolly… shit, I mean Becca. I'm Steven."

"I know your name," she answers, very politely. "You can save my life anytime you want. Avra has been talking about you. Yeah, sisters talk, even in encrypted messages."

"Really? What did she say?" I ask as Avra pretends not to be listening.

Cindy mumbles, "Here you go again, Stevie boy; don't make an ass of yourself."

"Haha, she said you are an adorably sexy fuck-up who just happened to save her life," Becca replies.

"She told you that?" I ask, raising my eyebrows.

"Which part?" she responds

"That I was a fuck-up?"

Smiling coyly, Becca says, "No, actually she said you were starting to get to her."

"Whaddaya mean?" I desperately ask.

"Um, like turning her on," she coyly replies, as Avra's skin reddens as though she was a preteen.

"Ha, Avra, love when you blush," I say with a huge grin.

"Stop it," Avra demands.

I am so gone—lock, stock, and barrel. Oh man—can never figure out females—drive you crazy or break your heart.

"Ok, enough of this junior high school stuff, let's get the fuck out of here and rendezvous back at the safe house," Avra says like she's in charge.

"Where's what's his name?" I ask.

"Ya mean Holtzmann?" Becca asks meekly. "Oh yeah… well, he sends his regrets for the shindig, but he did leave this little party favor." She holds up a tiny black object.

"What's that?" I ask.

"His black hole, Steven," she replies like I'm supposed to know. "That's his research and data—yep, that's it—gonna keep it safe right here in my back pocket. This is going to save the world," patting her backside.

"Your butt?" I ask, grinning ear to ear.

"No silly, the black hole," she responds.

"Well, where is he?" I prod.

"Um, hm–ah… still in the cave… yes, he is," Becca states firmly.

"Cave? What the fuck? What's he doing?" I ask.

"Well, ah, he's sleeping," she says.

"Sleeping? Whaddaya talkin' about?" I probe incredulously.

"Ah, so, uh, well, he had a headache and um, he ah… Di-didn't Avra tell you? …Avra?" Becca's looking at her sister and raising her eyebrows.

Avra just shrugs her shoulders and smirks.

"This is going to be a real shocker," Cindy whispers.

"Duh?" Becca, hands on her hips, furrows her eyebrows.

"Tell me what?" I ask, like a moron.

"Ok Stevie, remember I said there is some more to tell you—ya know—like the rest of the story?" Avra responds. "Listen, ah, everything I told you is the truth… but I ah, didn't tell you every little itsy-bitsy detail."

This whole charade is really starting to piss me off, even with these glorious sexy bodies surrounding me.

"Stop playing games," I demand. "What the fuck are you talking about—details?"

"Be careful, Stevie boy, you're treading on thin ice," Cindy warns. "Don't ever ask a question that you don't know the answer to, like all those smart lawyers out there."

"Well, sort of sleeping… ah, yeah… likes to sleep… was up late last night," Becca states.

"Hey, it's almost noon—get him up!" I order.

"He won't get up," she says very doggedly.

"Why, why-the-fuck-not?" I ask desperately.

"He-ah, um, really can't," Becca says.

"Are you girls nuts? You're talking gibberish," I'm looking at both as if they're crazy.

"So, ya know that headache?" Becca continues.

"Yeah?"

"It was a bad one," she says, shaking her head sorrowfully.

"Like a migraine?" I wonder.

"Worse, much worse." She answers with a long sigh.

"Maybe he has a brain tumor," I suggest.

"No… I, I really don't think so, something else for sure," she states.

"Then what? …need to extract him… get him home," I'm starting to shout.

"That's not going to happen, Steven," she says firmly.

"Why not?" demanding more than I am receiving.

"Well, ya know that headache I was talking about?" Becca, hands back on hips, rolls her eyes.

"Yeah, yeah… maybe he needs some medication or something," I suggest.

"Um… I um… don't think that'll help," Avra piped up.

"Why not?" I yell, getting fed up with this bullshit.

Becca answers, "So, I… I know the cause of… of his headache."

"Ya do?" I quiz her.

"Yes, I do."

"What?" I yell.

"He has a hole in his temple," Becca states.

"Ya mean ah… like his synagogue?" I ask.

"No, Steven—he has a real hole," Avra says flatly.

"Yikes, how did he get a hole?" shaking my head in disbelief.

"My little sister shot him," Avra declares, as if I should've known this the whole time.

"That would be me." Becca raises her hand and smiles.

"You shot him? —you fucking shot him?" I scream.

"Yep… blasted a 9 mm from one side of his head to the other, yes, I did." Becca says, very matter-of-factly.

"Dead?" I ask, frantically.

"Yessiree. He certainly is—not awake—for sure. Holtzmann Viktor is dead... gonzo," Becca repeats.

"That's why I had to vacate the cave so fast… needed to go stealth temporarily just in case they were monitoring me. Had no choice. Sorry to scare everyone," Becca says meekly.

"Yeah. At first," Avra whispers with concern, "we didn't know what happened… very nervous. Lost communication, but it was you who shut it down intentionally. Perfect. *'SIGH.'* Always some drama with this secret agent stuff. Crazy. Good job, little sistah!!" giving Becca a high five and a double fist pump.

"Holy shit, motherfucker, Goddamn Jesus fucking Christ— Viktor? Why Viktor? Why the fuck did you kill him? Goddamn fuckin' A. We are so screwed. Fuuuuuuuuuuuuuuk!" I scream.

"Steven—relax," Cindy wisely tells me. "This mission ain't over yet... 'not till the fat lady sings.'"

Chapter 57

"Here goes, the whole truth and nothing but the truth… but ya know, Stevie boy," Avra explains, "you can't handle the truth."

"Try me—I'm on your side—remember? Came from your people—our people—we are one."

Using another abandoned trail, so as not to repeat ourselves if anyone is tracking us, we go deeper into the woods. Dense and remote, but sanctuary-like, with moss-covered oak and fir. Ferns trying to make their presence felt, create a meditative retreat to comfort the souls walking in nature. We begin our journey home.

"Yeah, you want the facts?" Avra asks. "Well, get ready, here they are. Becca, why don't you fill in the blanks for our cute little Cleveland Heights friend as we trek back to the safe house and retrieve the Jeep."

So finally, Becca explains the genesis of her mission. About ten years ago, she journeyed to Russia on a student visa to pursue piano training with the foremost teacher in the world—a master bitch, Professor Maria Nikolaevna, descendant of the famous Grand Duchess of the same name. It was Becca's dream to be the best. But as the real story goes, she is, and always will be a Mossad agent. The real mission was to befriend Dr. Holtzmann Viktor, turn him into a spy, and establish a conduit into the new Russian nuclear program. You can't make this shit up.

Right off the bat, he was infatuated with her. Maybe it was her ability to perfectly play Bach's Praeludium in C major, or possibly the gentle kindness that she offered to this troubled but brilliant soul.

"Most likely, it was my slow, exotic, pulsating blow jobs that induced him to acquiesce," Becca says straight up. "In the end, it really didn't matter—he was mine—I nailed him."

Oh my God, it's impossible to focus on anything else after that. Goddamn. Staring at her lips, I can't get past the blowjob part—but Cindy says she's gonna quiz me on the rest of the story.

Anyway, Viktor confided in her about the historic black hole discoveries and even demonstrated them in his secret lab. He was so proud. Her commanders were even more ecstatic.

It was a monumental love story, although fabricated by a double agent on a mission. The good Professor enjoyed wonderful interludes with Becca playing the piano and himself discussing his groundbreaking discoveries. She reported every detail back to the people at King David, and it became obvious, as time progressed, that not only was he a sociopath, but in reality, a paranoid schizophrenic and extremely delusional. He kept hearing voices—sometimes they would be Stalin's—other times, his teachers constantly berating him.

The voices that bothered him the most were those of his parents—blaming him for surviving, and then ordering him to seek revenge, first against the Russian government, but later—anybody in authority.

"He told me," Becca confesses, "'They all must suffer and die an agonizing death—everyone, everyone, everyone,' he repeated over and over again. Ha, there was no better choice: thermal nuclear heat or radiation poisoning. Near the end, he just wanted to nuke everybody—good and evil—couldn't differentiate. Totally bonkers—I was his only salvation—his sanctuary. Don't know whether it was his way to offset his hallucinations or maybe he just found some inner sanctum with me."

"It gets better, Stevie boy—pay attention," Cindy chuckles as only she can.

Over time, her mission morphed. No longer was it just spy stuff—now it was extraction and termination. Her orders were specific: secure and conceal the hard drive; leave Russia with the data and... Viktor in tow. Once they were safe, Holtzmann would be eliminated.

As the plot thickens and the story unfolds, I get very upset.

"Take it easy Steven." Cindy intervenes. "Don't say anything you'll regret. Think about her tits and butt crack," she points out. "Don't mess this up; you're in a great position. Remember, you were chosen."

I just sigh and smile. Cindy is right, Goddamnit. She's always fucking right.

According to Becca, killing him was the easy part; the real problem was getting access to the hard drive which he secretly hid. She was the only one who knew of its existence—so she had to be damn sure it was the singular copy with no redundancies. Viktor knew that if the Russians discovered it… sayonara. He was so paranoid at the end that Becca was convinced no other copy existed. The only option was to get him out of the country with the hard drive. Then— and only then—would she be able to successfully resolve and conclude the mission. Crazy shit.

Holtzmann was allowed to travel to international seminars and scientific meetings—but never with his computer. His last paper, "The Relationship of Fragmented Quarks to the Theory of Chaos," was presented in Paris, but the information was electronically forwarded prior to the meeting to eliminate the need for his laptop or any electronic devices. The Russians were as paranoid as he was—a match made in Hell. Amazingly, he sincerely trusted her, so she told him to bring the hard drive because they wouldn't be returning.

"I'm not sure if he really understood the consequences of this new reality, but he woefully needed me for his last vestige of sanity. I was his only solace, so—he acquiesced to my request." She sighs.

Holtzmann invented a way to self-contain the drive into a fountain pen… ingenious… but of course, he was Holtzmann. At these conferences, she was always his escort, along with several out-of-shape ex-KGB bodyguards who liked to drink more than guard. They were no match for this little 'shayna maidela.'

On the last night of the conference, after the presentation, they went out to a tiny French restaurant on the Left Bank. Becca drugged the bodyguards' vodkas, and then took off—all planned out to perfection. This had to happen quickly. One of our agents on the ground drove them to the mountains after circling and changing vehicles four times. The last one was a super-charged, off-road Mercedes Safari fucking monster—like a tank. By the time anyone realized, they were long gone.

The bottom line—Holtzmann wanted to die—it was his only redemption, and he trusted her implicitly. She was his saint—his 'Stairway to Heaven.' He was a complete and total danger to society—there was no other way. So, in the end—although it's always difficult for someone to fulfill a personal termination contract, Becca knew it had to be done, and he consented. This was the best path to truly go home, attain peace, and be with his family for eternity. He agreed—with all his heart.

"Lovingly, he opened the pen and gave me the hard drive," Becca sadly recounts. "Serenely looking into my eyes, Holtzmann, smiling his last smile, asked that I kiss his capella… his forehead. I remember hearing Yo-Yo Ma playing Bach's 'Praeludium.'"

Chapter 58

Beethoven tells you what it's like to be Beethoven
and Mozart tells you what it's like to be human.
Bach tells you what it's like to be in the universe.
— *Douglas Adams*

As we emerge from the woods in the Jeep, the house appears in the distance and seems to call out, "Welcome home." What a perfect ending. We need to celebrate.

Moishe, Zelig, Raffi, Avra, Becca, and I, yearning for the sovereignty and warmth of our five-century old sanctuary, finally return home. Since our last visit, there have been many resolutions for me: I have become a man, a soldier, and a comrade—and have secured my demons, at least for now. Above all, this special girl has empowered me to be the best I can be. I smile internally.

Entering the magnificent front door with the required solemnity, we all embrace the beckoning of our heritage and ask ourselves, as Golda Meir said to Anwar Sadat, 'What took you so long?' Indeed, we answered the call.

Re-creating the previous special shindig would be difficult— but why not try? We all help to prepare the final banquet—a farewell orgasmic dining orgy. While the previous bash is an incredibly magnificent memory, and it's never easy to improve upon perfection, we give it our best shot. Who knows? This celebration may establish quite different musings that could become even more special.

The rest is history. Here goes:

Instead of fresh fish, we invite a couple of interested rabbits to join the simmering pot of stew with the freshest rosemary just plucked in the garden. We throw in some potatoes, turnips, parsley, and cabbage that we harvested from our special garden. While it's cooking, we indulge in some extraordinary local white wines specially aged and always available for us. By the time our feast is ready to enjoy, we are seriously buzzed. We save a few bottles of the sacred red wine to wash our palates and embrace this marvelous feast.

What a way to celebrate a successful mission and the death of the once-great scientist—very macabre. According to many religions and customs—life and death are really the same. 'Life has no beginning and has no end.' has been preached for millennia by many cultures. However, most people would rather stay alive and be with their loved ones in the same metaverse.

Toasting each other, "L'chaim—to life—to love—to live."

Okay, I'm ready—so ready—I want her—need her—but will I be able to close the deal? Cindy knows, but she's not talking; won't even look in my direction... not a good sign.

C'mon Dolly, I'm asking for your help—please—demanding your assistance—Cindy Buckaroo. After all I've done: rescued you, protected you, shielded you, and put up with your fucking bullshit and freaking hormonal rants. It's time for me to cash in the chips, take the money off the table, and enjoy the fruits of my success.

Moishe has been observing all dinner and suddenly gets up and says, "C'mon boychik—take a walk with me while I finish this cigar. Let's go, sonny boy—gotta couple of things to discuss."

I follow him out the back door like a little puppy dog. Facing us is a perfect night—the brilliant star-filled sky that amazed our ancestors.

I can see it coming, a frickin' lecture.

"Well Stevie—I understand you earned your stripes; they're calling you a hero, a fucking hero." Then he screams at the top of his voice, "You could have killed her—do you understand, asshole? Do you? Then I would have had to rip your head off—if those fucking Islamic shit-faces hadn't already castrated your fucking balls. You acted without thinking," he's continuing to shriek at me. But then, smiling and putting his massive arms around my neck, "Haha, boychik, you also executed your duty without fear." Grabbing me in a suffocating bear hug, he softly whispers, "That's the sign of a true warrior—ya can't teach that stuff; either you're born with it or you're not, and you've got it in your Jewish scrotum," as he gently kisses my cheek.

"Now for the second topic—don't ever, ever hurt Avra," Moishe warns. "I don't mean physically because she'll kick the living shit out of you. Talking about breaking her heart; then I'll really get mad. She's crazy about you but ah—she won't ask you out on a date like the other girls nowadays, too proud, too busy fighting for her country. So, grab the brass ring and sweep her off her feet. That's what Avra wants. Go after her. She's your lifetime gift, damnit. Kiss her, hold her, love her—don't screw this up. You'll never get another perfect soulmate. Go for the gusto."

"How do you know about everything?" I ask in awe.

"I know, I know, just do it," he responds. "You're a Ranger, you're Mossad, and now you're a frickin' warrior. Go get her, Tiger—Carpe Diem!"

Chapter 59

Moishe and I quietly venture back as everyone is clearing the table and rejoicing in our imminent return to Israel. Becca is jumping out of her skin in excitement, not having been back for such a long time. Hopefully, no special-ops missions for a while.

With my heart racing, I count to three and saunter over to join the two sisters who are immersed in a giggling conversation about who knows what. Standing there for a few seconds, I quietly interrupt. "Hey Avra, wanna take a walk? It's delightful out there."

"Sure," she answers, with a slight grin.

So, we peacefully depart through the back portico and stroll for a few minutes in total silence enjoying the almighty Milky Way. As if on cue, I take her hand, reciting the sacred blessing, *Shehekianu*, thanking God for bringing us to this day. It's in our genes.

Looking into my eyes with a twinkle in hers, she whispers, "Let's make a wish."

Without pausing she begins:

Star light, star bright,

First star I see tonight,

I wish I may, I wish I might,

Have this wish I wish tonight.

Softly caressing my lips, she moans, "C'mon Stevie; it's time."

In the blink of an eye, the stars align. Our families become one. We unite to fulfill the dreams of those who came before us. Do you believe in miracles?

Avra places her cool hand gently on my sweaty neck and whispers, "Steven, welcome to my real world. Please come to bed. You were born and bred for me—you are mine, forever and always. Am Yisrael chai. The people of Israel live."

Chapter 60

There was a star riding through clouds one night,
& I said to the star, 'Consume me'.
— Virginia Woolf

My anticipation is sensually razor sharp. Seriously. Fuckin' A, son-of-bitch, you dog. Thinking back—how did a street kid from Cleveland Heights gravitate to this surreal moment?

Only got laid once and that was with a very charming prostitute who gave my buds and me a discount because she liked us. She also said I was the best looking.

Some back seat 'in-car' hand jobs from a cheerleader accounted for the bulk of my experience—but she was adorable. As a reward, she let me play with her pussy until it got slimy-wet and she started to moan, "Don't stop—don't ever stop."

Well, eventually I had to rest because I got a cramp in my arm. Anyway, that was it. She wouldn't let me stick my guy in her twat because she was Catholic, probably rationalized she wasn't really sinning, so, to her credit, she remained a virgin. I begged her, but to no avail. We repeated the automobile sex on multiple occasions until we both perfected our skills for the pleasure of our future spouses.

Meandering toward the rear portico leading to the master bedroom, Avra explains that it was originally the family chapel and later converted to a boudoir. The entryway is perfectly situated with a view of the mountains to the north and protected from the sun by a magnificent grape trellis of aged teak lattice.

After what seems like an eternity, we finally reach the resplendent oak doors which guard the sanctity of the chamber and our destination for the evening. Can't breathe—unable to speak. Massive panic is evolving but Avra and Cindy don't know. Staring at the mountains as if praying, paralyzed—fear of failure—terror. Get a hold of yourself, fucking asshole. Snap out of it! Dig deep—use all your power—let it out!

My Mom's voice comes into my head, 'you can do whatever you want—never in doubt—just do it!'

"Steven, you ok?" Avra quietly asks.

"Sure, just taking it all in. Everything is so strikingly gorgeous—especially you." I'm calmly smiling at her now.

Blushing, she nods to the doors. "Come, my precious warrior, let me show you the most astounding boudoir."

The chamber is like nothing I had ever encountered—truly mystical. Avra explains that the original owners in the Middle Ages were very religious Catholics who required the holiness of a church every day—so they built their own.

"My great, great, great-grandparents used it as their bedroom. Pretty cool, huh?"

The doorway reveals a pure, bright, rectangular space with vast open windows on three sides. There is a gentle breeze flowing from the west carrying the essence of cypress and juniper trees. The descending light is so clear and vibrant—capturing the electrifying sunset. Everything seems to be fantastical as in a 'Technicolor' animation.

The windows expose the expansive, glorious Pyrenees plain with the foreboding but protective mountains in the background. Eons of history and culture stare back. The prevailing breeze cleanses and restores the humble mortals fortunate enough to be healed by its therapeutic blessings. As the sun disappears behind the peaks, its magical spell comforts all the creatures. It is the golden hour—there is no evil in the world.

The outlines of the original chapel remain intact. The rounded ceiling displays a splendid but faded fresco by an unknown artist from the 1600s—a scene of angels frolicking in Heaven.

She guides me, Cindy in tow, as we enter the womb of this converted holy place. The boudoir—our sexually sacred bedroom—created by generations of kind people that shared this sanctuary, welcomes our union. There are layers of Avra's family and predecessors who consecrate our tiny instant of time, no matter how insignificant in the context of the expansive universe and beyond.

The tranquility of the moment produces a spiritual presence. Even Cindy is blown away as Avra maintains our privacy by firmly securing the centuries-old double church doors with an echoing thud—

encasing us in this time warp.

"Oh, fuck!" Cindy screams. "Oh, my God."

Not knowing what to say, I say nothing, just smile at my destiny girl. Avra turns slowly to me, whispering, "You will never forget this evening," as I feel my cock inching down my left thigh like a bon vivant snake out for an adventurous interlude.

Holy shit, I notice the majestic marble bathtub next to the palladium windows, there—for us. The indescribable basin, situated on a stone platform, is filled with bubbles, while a succulent bowl of local white grapes and two glasses of champagne anticipate our recital—what a performance it will be.

Avra hands me a pure white terry cloth robe and says, "Ok, Ranger, please remove your clothes and meet me by the love pot."

I just stand there in shock, watching her saunter around the corner of the bed to the stupendous open area shower. The original altar currently supports the magnificent four-poster oak frame that will be our love-nest for the evening. Would it be sacrilegious to engage in such activity on this conduit to God and those up above? Whatever.

"Wow, some safe house," I'm whispering to Cindy, who has been there for generations. She is taking it all in and enjoying the reunion.

I hesitantly remove my uniform of sorts, or what is left of it. Slowly and uneasily, detaching each piece of clothing until I get to my boxer shorts; I hate tighty-whities. Looking down, I see my old friend morph from a slinky snake to a robust totem pole seeking recognition.

Putting on my robe, I now resemble a tepee.

Is this embarrassing or what, especially from a secret black-ops killing machine? Avra's going to think I'm a novice—just act like you've been here before, asshole.

Making my way to the bubbles, grapes, and champagne, I suddenly realize that no matter what happens the rest of my life, my heart is full, my cup runneth over. Hearing rustling behind me, I turn to see the most ravishing view I have ever encountered. Avra appears from around the corner and stops. I can only stare in astonishment.

Never have my eyes focused on such pure splendor and strength of character. My brain tells me that this special woman possesses a face and body for the ages, but my heart perceives her inner joy and love which is the culmination of generations of powerful souls that present this glorious human vision… *bashert*… it was meant to be. Yes, Avra is my destiny—lover for whom I was born—the alignment of the sun, the moon, and stars create our spectacular reunion on Earth. The future is ours; the moment is now. The present is the present.

Avra blinks first and with just the slightest break of her lip, she beckons me to the bath as she peacefully whispers, "Steven, please cleanse me."

Ok, that sounds like a good idea—watching my love slowly slithering her robe to the ground as she glides her perfect body toward my enormous erection.

"Ha, Steven; looks like we have a lot of work to do," she says jokingly, but correct in her assumption.

"You can say that again," I whisper.

"What, darling?"

"Nothing."

Praying—please God, make me a star, a walk-off, grand slam, home run.

Her pitch-black hair, still moist from the shower, enticingly nips at the flawless nape of her elegant neck. The Venus of harmony provided by the convergence of her deliciously beckoning thighs surely replicates the most perfect goddess. I know exactly what she's doing—driving me crazy.

In slow motion and perfect unison, we lightly place our hands on each other's hips and gently draw together. Her hardened nipples desire more while the essence of her love juice mixes with the scent of the breeze from the fertile plane. Smiling, we both close our eyes, anticipating the ecstasy to come.

"Perimeter intrusion. Perimeter intrusion. Perimeter intrusion."

Instead, our peace is shattered by the painfully loud and ear-splitting alarm accompanied by harsh, flashing blue lights. What the hell is going on? Fuck! A synthesized female voice keeps blaring *"perimeter intrusion, perimeter intrusion,"* over and over and over again. Holy shit. I can't believe this is happening, just my luck—so close and yet so far.

"Critical incursion, Steven, this is the real deal!" she yells.

"Gotta get dressed and get the hell out of here to find out what intel knows. I promise you," kissing me on the cheek, "we shall reconvene somehow, somewhere, maybe in an altered state."

This is a disaster—not exactly what I was anticipating on this special night. Peering out the window, I can see a monster thunderstorm brewing in the distance coming this way. Stars are still apparent overhead, allowing functional satellite imagery for the time being. Nothing seems amiss, except for my dick, which is very confused. We are gonna get a huge cloudburst shortly—God knows what else.

Chapter 61

INTRUSION

"Initiate Code Jericho. Initiate Code Jericho!" Moishe screams on the PA system. "Go, Go, Go."

We open the doors just in time to see Zelig barreling by in full combat gear, ready for battle as the annoying and relentless intrusion alarm keeps screaming its maddening message.

"What the hell's going on, Avra? I've got Cindy." I gently place her in my rucksack.

"Keep moving and head down to the cellar," she yells.

The perimeter has been breached through the invisible electronic fence surrounding the internal five hundred acres. The place is lit up like it's Monday Night Football. Looking out the window, I can't see anybody. Lots of lightning in the distance; thunder delay is getting shorter—big storm's gonna hit soon—cameras and satellites are reporting a large platoon infiltrating from every direction. Not sure who they are, but most likely the radical Iranian Brigade. All hell is breaking loose.

Code Jericho is drilled weekly, but this is the Real McCoy. No amount of practice can simulate live action and the added anxiety that goes with it. Our whole team, my team, is very energized but looks calm, almost peaceful—all professionals.

"Move. Everyone, move. Downstairs, let's go; lock the metal door behind us," Raffi orders. "Steven—into the boiler room. Open the side of that monster; it's gutted. Step into it," he directs.

It's an old, walk-in boiler, originally coal-burning, a huge mama, not in use anymore. It has a false casing; the new high-tech one's on the other side of the house. Once inside the boiler, there's a very steep second set of stairs leading to another area. When everyone's safely down to the next level, Raffi and I seal the metal door behind us with a ratchet and a welding torch. It will slow 'em up a little bit, at least temporarily, we hope. Every second counts when people are trying to snuff you out. Memories of getting trapped in an old elevator in downtown Cleveland resurface. Sealing us in gives me a very uncomfortable claustrophobic feeling, like I'm being locked in a tomb or reliving the frickin' gondola nightmare:

Man, I was out of bounds with nowhere to hide, as my wacky red-haired partner encapsulated me in this grotesque steel cage. Shit. Felt like a mummy in a tomb with no way out. Fuck me. Panic was overwhelming my body.

Utilizing drones, our intel has identified the fanatical Iranian

Brigade as the antagonists. They are getting closer, and the huge storm is predicted to unleash its fury shortly. Historically, the valley floods quickly; the flash water is dangerous and deadly. I can sense more tension from the team as we hurry around the corner to the sub-cellar, and down more stairs, into an open room which looks like a parking lot. It's so big you could drive a bunch of semis in here. The Germans used it for everything: weapons, bomb shelter, and prisoners.

In the far corner—hot, new, red Peugeot MGP30 racing cycles—very sexy, but not as wicked as Avra's Indian Scout. They all have side scabbards with UZIs and a back storage compartment for hand grenades and Semtex. Five bikes for six people. *I am hoping it will be Avra and me on the same bike, so I make an executive decision and tell her to hop on the back of the nasty machine because this bad boy will be driving.*

Ha, I used to race my 400 Norton up and down High Street at OSU:

The 400cc Norton, vintage mid-sixties, was a work-horse machine and fun to drive. Built by the British, it had a driveshaft instead of a chain—very smooth and powerful. The best thing, or the worst, depending on your perspective, was the manual kick start—very retro and sometimes exhausting. It made you feel part of the cycle and wasn't for the faint of heart, or faint of breath, for that matter, but it sure was fun.

My buddy, Bruce, a ZBT fraternity brother, was a red-headed, freckled face, hard-ass motherfucker, and the exact opposite of Jabber; he never said a word unless it was important—just stared you down. Every evening at about midnight, when things just started to get going, he and I squeezed into our tight button-front Levi 501s, jumped into our cool Frye boots, slipped on Buckeye T-shirts, and headed to High Street on the Ohio State campus where the coeds were getting pretty juiced. Screeching up and down High, from the North Berg to the South Berg, we laid a lot of rubber powered by the cheers of the freshman girls and the boos of the senior guys. Great memory!

Grinning, Avra jumps on the back of the MGP and wraps her arms around me. "Cute butt," she whispers, softly.

'VROOM, VROOM,' the cycle howls!

"C'mon, you fuckers. Yahoo!" I yell. "This Army Ranger is leading the way. Code Jericho! Geronimo, whatever! Hang on tight, Avra, and never let go," screaming as I do a wheelie, down this mind-blowing tunnel, just like in Columbus. "Yoooha!"

Becca yells, "Haha. Well, I have his prize right here," patting her sexy, tight butt with the hard drive safely in her pocket. "Yahoohoohoo!"

Germans always had great technology; this massive subway is no exception. Over the years, everything in the tunnel was updated and maintained in case of a scenario like tonight. Fuck the Germans and fuck the Iranians, but sometimes, Moishe told me, it floods with heavy rains. Realizing that is a possibility, I start wondering what would be worse than getting sealed in this tunnel? The answer is getting trapped in a tunnel with water.

An intel update reports that troops are surrounding the house and the storm is moving in. Satellite imagery will be lost soon. It's suspected that Garf Zeman himself is here. They're desperate to get Viktor, thinking he is still alive, but his technology's the real trophy— and they don't even know about the black hole miniaturization.

What a fucking piece of engineering. Hell of a corridor.

Whoa! Internal camera surveillance is telling us they're inside and ripping the house apart. Just a matter of time before they find the boiler and blow the door.

"Hurry, step on it!" Zelig yells. "Faster." We all downshift and accelerate as fast as the cycles will go.

VROOM... VROOM...

It must be pouring outside because water starts to seep in along the walls. The ventilation is beginning to drip. Now—more water, about an inch as we pass a curve where the tunnel starts to reverse-trek at a 5% vertical incline up to the mountains. There's a massive door at that junction that'll be sealed shut once we get through and head up. Water's really starting to pour in here. We're about two miles from the house and can hear the devastating storm outside.

VROOM... VROOM...

Downshifting past the opening—we all stop and jump off. It's time to close the enormous vault-like entrance, now behind us. It's three feet of solid concrete, reinforced with Kevlar, weighing about five tons, but not impenetrable. Anything can be opened with the right equipment, even Fort Knox—but it'll slow the bastards a little. Meanwhile, the water penetration accelerates, increasing the depth from one to three inches in a matter of minutes.

CLANK! THUD!

Zelig, Moishe, and I slowly seal the enormous door behind us.

The wheel-like mechanism with its core projections extends into the tunnel frame, locking us out or in—depending on your perspective.

The immediate problem is the water pouring down the incline. Looks like Niagara Falls. Focusing on the vault as it seals us out—claustrophobia tries to emerge, but there's no looking back, only forward. The influx of water is rapidly accelerating. We have to get to the next doorway before the tunnel floods or we will be totally submerged with no way out. Fuck me, as I think of the agonizing helo dunker:

The dunker sank as the water replaced the air. Turned over upside down. ...can't breathe. ...drowning. Panic hit—then and now.

"Everyone, follow us with the cycles; don't stop," Avra screams as she squeezes me tight.

The water depth is now at least six inches and rising. The Peugeots will be useless in a few minutes, and the terrorists are closing in fast. This is far worse than any of the Ranger training. This is real! If we don't escape this section of the tunnel before it totally floods, we'll be fucked. Can't go back because the door is sealed, and the Iranians are on the other side. We have to move forward as fast as possible and get to the next level. No other options available; it would be a slow death by drowning when the water level rises to the ceiling. Killed by terrorist weapons or drowning in a German-made tunnel— not good options. Intelligence updates are pouring in almost as fast as the water, indicating they found the boiler and are trying to blow it.

"About time they figured it out," Avra says. "Stupid fucks. Hurry! Hurry! Shit!"

...may have to ditch the bikes if the water gets any deeper. I can't show weakness; I must hold it together. Don't like this; could get trapped. Ooh, man!

The cycles are starting to sputter and stall; water getting into the engines. *Goddamnit. Fuck! These souped-up bikes are about done. It will be very difficult and time-consuming walking in the water, like trying to march in deep ocean surf—almost impossible.*

Like a choreographed dance, every Peugeot conks out in rapid succession... drowning in the rushing water. They won't restart. We have to hoof it the rest of the way if we don't drown first. Oh God, starting to feel the tension build in my body, remembering the water survival test:

Gasping for air. Going to fucking croak. Didn't want to die.

Please don't let me die here.

Under water. Choking. Pissing.

Moishe's screams bring me back to reality. "Hurry! Fuck the bikes; run the rest of the way. Let's go—or we'll drown."

It's utterly grueling trying to run and high-step-it in the water, which is now over our knees. Everything is falling apart. Can't believe this is happening, my worst nightmare; my heart's exploding. We walk and run for what feels like a marathon—probably only a few hundred yards—but we're exhausted, gasping for air, trying to catch our breath. Seems like miles to go... no end in sight.

Cindy keeps telling me to look inward, maybe there's something we're missing. They all knew about the possibility of flooding, and the team had been talking about all the upgrades to the tunnel. There have to be provisions for emergency situations. Protocols and equipment for these eventualities must have been accounted for. Every fucking tunnel in the world has disaster gear. There are little red signs, strategically placed, labeling small niches for emergencies. What we really need is a fucking boat, but that's wishful thinking. Immediately, Cindy perks up.

Nobody here is familiar with the intricate schematics of the tunnel infrastructure. For better or worse, they never had the need to use the information in real time. A yearly scheduled maintenance is performed, but never a mention of emergency protocols for flooding, considering the frequency of flash floods in the area... has to be something. I ask Moishe if he could access the schematics from his gizmo watch. He can.

Sure enough, hidden on the last page: Contents of emergency alcove—fire extinguisher, phone, ax, and there it is—*inflatable boat,* Cindy's fucking boat—she knew it all along! This could be a game changer, a life-saving event to get us to the exit and avoid death by drowning. The next red emergency sign is just ahead. High stepping through the waves, I open the door, exhausted. The cabinet is not well lit, so I take out my flashlight and peer inside. As specified, there are a fire extinguisher, an AED, and an ax, but where is the boat? Fuck. According to the specs, still about a mile to go until the portal exit, right after the next switch up. The water is rising so fast that the only way to survive is by using a boat.

I rip everything out of the storage area to recheck the components, and, on the bottom in the corner is a small square package, wrapped in plastic with a picture of the boat, Cindy's beautiful little boat.

The packaging label gives instructions on how to inflate it and specifies a maximum of six people. Perfect.

Moishe rips apart the covering and desperately looks for the red pull cord to initiate inflation. There it is, on the reverse edge, a simple, little, red cable loop that says in Hebrew, "pull to inflate." He grabs it and yanks on the cord—nothing. He pulls again—same result. Again, and again. It's fucking broken.

"Blow it up by mouth, our mouths," I order, as I grab the

stubborn, deflated boat, look for the orifice which is part of the auto-inflation mechanism, and start blowing my brains out. I blow and blow and blow until I become dizzy. Zelig takes over and does the same until he turns blue in the face. Our little boat is growing before our eyes just like a little boy as he gets older. It's Moishe's turn as he places the nipple-like structure in his mouth and blows his guts until he almost passes out. The boat is almost ready to float; it needs one more set of young, healthy lungs and those belong to Avra. She places the orifice in her mouth, and everybody yells, "Blow, blow, blow."

'The little boat that could' is born—a beautiful, little, blue baby boat that's going to save our lives.

Everybody's so excited until we realize that there are no paddles or any other means of navigation. The inflatable apparatus is just designed to float, not to travel. Shit, how are we going to voyage upstream and get to the exit? Water is getting higher, now over our waists. What the fuck are we gonna do? We are truly up the creek without a paddle.

Noticing that the rig is much longer than wide, I figure that if we turn the boat sideways, maybe it will be wide enough to use our hands against the walls to generate traction and leverage forward. It won't be as efficient as lengthwise navigation, but it's our only chance. I instruct everybody to rotate the raft 90°, with two guys and a girl on each end. We also take the long-handled ax.

Using our hands against the walls, we push back to allow the boat to go forward and keep repeating this motion. At first, we're not moving much because our strokes are not in unison.

"We need to synchronize our motion like a racing scull crew. Everyone has to push at the exact same time. Push, push, push!" I yell like a coxswain.

It's beginning to work; we're moving forward. "Push, push, push!" we all scream together. It's happening. At first slowly, but then we build up a little more speed as we make headway against the current coming down the incline. We are like a finely-tuned Olympic team competing for a gold medal.

I was a kid who always went my own way, away from the maddening crowd—or the bird who flies from the flock in another direction. Now I know what the Chinook salmon must feel like when they journey hundreds of miles upstream, jumping currents and waterfalls to propagate their species. "Push, push, push!" We root each other on.

Again and again, we stroke against the walls, but we're so exhausted—like running a marathon, but will we cross the finish line?

Remembering my great football coach, Ray Warner, who motivated me to run faster by increasing the intensity of my wind sprint ... "Dig, dig, dig!" he yelled, until I was ready to throw up.

We can see the steel door ahead of us as I look around at my colleagues. Moishe and Raffi are gasping for air, on their way to heart attacks, while Zelig, who is in great shape, is hanging in but struggling. The Ironwomen champions, Avra and Becca, dominate. The group, some in better shape than others, maintains unity, choreographed like a Russian ballet. It's gratifying to watch. We are a formidable team and cross the finish line together—cheering and crying.

Chapter 62

Conquer your fears, one fear at a time, and
eventually you will reach the finish line.
— Jeanette Coron

So out of breath... can hardly talk as we disembark from our little boat that could. Safety and freedom are just past the door. Zelig is first to reach the exit and tries to open the wheel hatch.

"AHHHHH. Damn. It's stuck," he yells.

"What do you mean, stuck? What's wrong?" I ask, freaking out.

"Rusted shut after all these years. Won't budge," he says.

Panic sets in for everybody, not just me. We all push… no dice. The water level's quickly rising; don't have much time. Can't get out. Remembering that terror of the helo dunker, like a horror film. Shit.

Wow. Can feel that fear. Fucking scared. Claustrophobic. Shit. Trapped—like a mummy in a tomb with no way out.

Aware that I'm on the verge of losing it, Avra grabs my arm and kisses me on the cheek. "We'll be okay; we have to be," she promises. "There are so many things we *must* accomplish together."

So, here I am—a grown man, a fearless soldier with an eyeless doll, about to die in a Godforsaken tunnel in the middle of the Pyrenees. Impossible to fathom this discombobulated situation—I take a deep breath—must refocus. We keep trying to open the door to no avail. Looks really corroded—have to be careful not to break the mechanism. We can't blow it with the C-4... too dangerous and difficult to control in this enclosed space.

Cindy, naturally, is very upset like the rest of us and keeps telling me to look inward. "Look. Look. Look!" she is frantically telling me.

Never heard her yell before. Can't understand what she means, but she is very persistent. On some level, her thoughts are entering my mind... can't make sense of what she is telling me. Am I crazy or what?

Desperately seeking a solution, an idea comes to me. Maybe... opening the backpack and peering inside. There it is, right next to Cindy, my little travel can of WD-40. *Don't leave home without it.* You never know when it will come in handy, especially if you're a closet claustrophobic. Ha. "Thanks, C."

She knows everything.

Grabbing the famous lubricant, I squirt some on the rusted mechanism and let it soak in. "Try it now," I order.

"AHHHHHHHH!" Moishe yells. "Won't budge. Fuck."

"Wait a few seconds; let it do its job," I plead. "Never fails."

Raffi begs for us to hurry as he starts to hyperventilate. The water is over our waist, and everybody looks terrified. The wheel is shoulder high, but if the water gets above that level we'll be sunk. No way to spritz WD under water.

Trying to calm the team down, I tell them I'm a master of anxiety; just focus on the door. Imagine me coaching others to relax. Yikes, Raffi's starting to lose it; I try to calm him down, knowing what he's going through—I'm an expert.

Sometimes it takes a few squirts to have this shit soak in, so I flood it and try again—nothing.

"Goddamnit, not moving. We're going to die in this fuckin' German tunnel. They don't even need to gas us!" Moishe yells.

Again, spritzing and attempting to loosen the latch even a little, the water's inches away from the lever, almost to our shoulders... nothing.

"Let me at that fucker!" I yell, pushing them aside.

The can is almost empty. Might as well give it everything until it's under water. No reason to save it now. "Use it or lose it," Cindy pipes up, so I empty the entire contents. All gone. The water's now above our shoulders and covering the latch. Becca jumps on Zelig's back to keep from drowning. Avra does the same with Moishe, like when we were kids. This, however, is not fun. Raffi's a basket case; no help at all. Fuck.

Oh man, we're hoping the Iranians blow the second door, the huge vault, so it would release the water. No dice. It's now up to me and Cindy. I promise her that if we ever get out of this predicament alive, she can have a hairdo and a new bunting. That's the least I can do; she really needs it.

Strangely wondering if Garf Zeman is in the tunnel, directing the action? Probably is. Maybe he knows we're drowning and doesn't want to open that end. Let nature kill us. Wouldn't put it past the sadistic fucker.

Time is not on our side, but all I can think of is the great Chambers Brothers' song, "The Time Has Come Today." This is our last chance. Will the WD-40 work? Will we survive? Will Avra and I finally fuck?

I swim to the door with Cindy in my waterproof backpack. You never know when you're going to need the best gear, but when you do, you've got it! Too bad Jabber isn't here. He insisted that we buy this high-end rucksack. Thanks, man! Cindy is copacetic, even while the water's rising above our shoulders.

The WD-40 is trying to do its job under water. Pushing as hard as possible, I feel a slight movement. Just a touch; it's something, but it won't go any further. The water is up to our necks. It's peculiar that I'm so serene. Maybe it's Cindy or the look of horror in Avra's eyes. What a way to die, but better than being shot by Zeman. Please God, let me do this! Need something for leverage.

...remembering from the 'live fire' drill using the pole to gain mechanical advantage to lift me out of the mud gunk... maybe we can use the ax handle like a car jack.

Grabbing the business head of the ax, I wedge it into the spoke of the latch wheel until secure and then try to rotate the mechanism—just like Sister Shelley taught. Force amplification at its finest! Mister

Wizard would be proud. Maybe I should introduce them one fine day—if we ever get out of here. Cindy could chaperone.

Wiggle. Wiggle. More movement.

Moving a touch. Everyone is praying. Pathetic.

Pushing again and again on the ax handle.

Nothing. Just anguish.

Breathing in to capture the last remnants of air, I scream, "Please open. Please!"

Cindy is at peace.

I hear thunder outside. The storm is raging. Fuck.

One last attempt. Trying as hard as I can, shrieking, "AHHHHHHHHHHHHHHH!!!"

Moving... moving... a little more... Please!

A little bit. We're almost there, feeling a slight clicking as the latch wheel miraculously disengages from the locking mechanism. WD-40 works under water. Can't wait to tell my Navy Seal buds, this could be a game changer. Betcha the WD company doesn't even know about the underwater possibilities. Could double their revenue, maybe even triple.

Whoa, I could be their worldwide rep. Oh man, TV, social media, billboards. Holy shit, Avra, Cindy, and me—now that's an A team. We'll go on the road, private jet, or our own million-dollar RV with a hot tub. Go anywhere, anytime, whatever the fuck we want.

We all cheer as a team—the family—we will always be.

It's unlocked, but now we have to open the door. Which way

does it go? Out or in? If it's in, we are screwed. The water pressure will never allow it.

No choice, it has to open out or we'll be dead in a few minutes.

Push, motherfucker, I will myself, "AHHHHHHHHH."

"With all your might," Cindy screams.

Hearing my mom, "Whatever it takes. *No* is not in your vocabulary."

A miracle. It opens out, and the water rips by us like rapids in the Niagara River at the brink of the falls. We are all pulled along with the torrent, bouncing against the steel and concrete exit with no way to protect ourselves.

Then there is tranquility.

The raging river is now a peaceful stream meandering through the concrete out into the woods. Emerging from the catacombs of despair, Raffi is Raffi again, laughing hysterically. Everyone is cheering for the right to breathe refreshing air. The rain has stopped. We are in a charming magical garden of ferns; the smell of jasmine permeates our heightened senses.

"You're right, Stevie, Army Ranger training is pretty damn good," Avra proudly tells me, grinning. "You're so strong and smart," grabbing my biceps and wooing me like a teenager—"my WD-40 guy. Think I need a lube job, Steven."

"You can say that again, ha! But I need to get another can."

Avra just rolls her eyes and chuckles. Maybe that's a good sign.

Looking to my right—there it is, where we left it earlier, next to the overgrown German concrete structure, Avra's sexy 'Indian Scout' racer.

"You devil you," I exclaim. "Good job," hugging her and rubbing her ass. "You knew all along this could be our escape. 'Code fucking Jericho.' Goddamn, son-of-a-bitch. Booya!"

"Stevie, why don't you drive the Indian, for old times' sake and for Jonny? I'll hop on back," she says.

Sitting on the Scout with Avra so close gives me an appreciation of fulfillment I've never felt before—a mindfucker.

VROOM... VROOM...

Throttling up and revving the engine so loud that maybe Jonny can hear—we make our way to a nearby escarpment allowing us to view the property directly. The others are right behind on foot. Moishe reports that most of the motherfuckers are still in the house and the tunnel with a few guarding outside. One of those is Garf Zeman. He is there—positively ID'd through facial recognition. The guy should rot in Hell; maybe this will be his day of reckoning.

"Ready?" Avra asks the group.

"Do it!" Zelig commands.

Avra enters the code into her Dick Tracy special watch: *#BAT.BUCKEYEMAMA.CHHS.TIGERS.*

A series of perimeter explosions erupts and destroys everything in its wake, including Avra's glorious home. In addition, napalm is released into the tunnel to fry all the cockroaches and the hundred-plus terrorist motherfuckers without destroying the irreplaceable German subway. Napalm, made famous in Viet Nam, was used extensively in every war beginning in WWII. It is a deadly incendiary weapon that brings back the famous line:

I love the smell of napalm in the morning.

— Apocalypse Now

Chapter 63

The Earth explodes right before our eyes. Holy shit. Awesome. Goddamn… wow. So, this is fucking 'Code Jericho.' Glad to be a part of it. Can't wait to tell my ole buds from Ranger School! Kinda wish Jabber could see this, but then I'd kill him again, that fucking traitor.

Silence erupts from the chaos—the explosions cease to exist, just smoke and fog.

Barely visible over the mountains, the sunrise begins its therapeutic journey to greet the lucky inhabitants of the magnificent Ariège plains. The violent storm of the past gives way to the promise of a spectacular day.

At the crack of dawn, our team takes off in a black SUV support vehicle hidden in the woods, leaving Avra and me alone—with her Indian motorcycle. We will all reconnoiter later in Marseille.

"Can't believe you destroyed your precious villa! The Mossad is really nuts," I declare in astonishment.

"Oh, Steven," Avra replies, "that building was a fake, a facsimile. The original burnt down years ago from a fire of unknown origin. The land is what really matters. Houses can be rebuilt—lives can't," as she hugs me so hard it hurts. "The German tunnel, on the other hand, would be very difficult to reconstruct. It was purposely not blown—could always be used for a future 'Code Jericho.'"

She explains that they made a replica just like Disneyland does. As it turns out, the stone and stucco are really Dryvit, a material that you can do just about anything with. Wire mesh covers a sprayed-on synthetic stucco, miracle product. Even the butcher blocks were fakes. The original paintings and frescoes were taken down a long time ago and archived in Israel years before the fire. She was always afraid that something could happen to them.

"People will speculate, 'it was a gas explosion from the flood—what a terrible accident!' Then, we will re-create it again," Avra proudly exclaims. "The fucking crazy terrorists will keep coming back, and we'll keep killing them."

Flabbergasted, I admit, "You had me fooled; the house sure looked authentic, but I was only focused on you." I share my truth as we gently touched cheeks and bodies. Tenderly whispering into her ear, "I love you Avra—you're my whole life," I'm feeling a massive hard-on emerging from the depths of my innards.

"I love you too, Ranger Steven," as she ever-so-lightly flicks her hand down the front of my pants—and I moan.

"Oh my God, can't live without you, Avra. Where's our next mission?" I'm barely able to speak.

"Ha... glad you asked," she's replying breathlessly as my hand slips down under her fatigues. "Cyprus is our next adventure; gonna be intense—be there—Stevie boy!" she orders.

"Are you kidding me? Wouldn't miss it for the world." Now I'm slowly unbuttoning her shirt, gently kissing her delicious lips.

The sun hurls dappled rays through the forest canopy as we become one person, uniting our souls for eternity.

As the way is circular, it has no beginning and no ending.

As it has no beginning and no ending, it is unlimited and infinite.

As it is unlimited, it has no roots and no branches.

Having no limits, it is neither wide nor narrow, with no concept of movement, pause, forwards, backwards, exterior or interior. It is identical, with no changing features and no different faces.

It is emptiness.

— Taisen Deshimaru

EPILOGUE

"Get up Steven. Get up."

"Wha... ?"

"Football practice. You'll be late." Mom is yelling from downstairs. "Making breakfast, need to eat," she pleads.

"Ok, ok," trying to focus. "Be right down," staring at the Eiffel tower between my legs.

"Ma, I was having an incredible dream," I say enthusiastically.

"Dream on, my son, but first you must eat," she orders.

AUTHOR'S NOTE

Writing and researching "Altered State of Affairs," created many poignant moments for me:

I discovered that my ancestors lived in Spain just like Avra's and experienced similar horrors. They were also expelled in 1492 but migrated to Kiev (now Kyiv) in Ukraine. Thriving in a small town or 'shtetl' called Tetiev, they lived peacefully for hundreds of years. Shortly before the pogroms of 1919 to 1920, my grandparents and many of their relatives came to the United States of America through Ellis Island and settled in Cleveland, Ohio. They were the lucky ones. Interestingly, the majority of Tetievers, as they are called, went to Cleveland to begin their new lives. My mother, born in 1919 in Cleveland, had four older siblings who were born in Kiev and emigrated here. Most of the fifteen hundred Jews who remained in Titiev were massacred. There were scores of similar towns in the Kiev region that have their own horror stories.

Parts of Avra's dialogue, edited out of the story for various reasons, are too important to lose entirely. I include her own words here:

"They were an integral component of the Spanish culture and way of life. My people resided in the province of Catalonia, near Barcelona. We thrived there—it was a wonderful time—but it didn't last. In 1492, the famous 'Alhambra Decree,' or edict of expulsion, evicted every single Jew.

"We were well educated. We owned homes and held respected positions: bankers, teachers, merchants, doctors. We were for the most part, fairly affluent. Ostensibly, that was the problem—always has been. We were the money people and the decision-makers but were perceived for 5,000 years as the troublemakers and ultimately the scapegoats— descendants from Hell. It is our curse and our blessing— we're 'the chosen,' but reviled. This was and is an unbearable, paradoxical burden. No other people in history have been shackled with our guilt and pain. Why are we hated? Why?

"That is not the reason for our discussion tonight. We are more concerned with real-time terrorist assaults directed at our present-day culture. Children are taught to despise and murder us—but also to fear and respect our ability to defend and survive. They want us dead—always have.

"Over the years, everyone has attempted to kill us, incinerate our flesh, and bury our culture, but we have persevered. Fucking Adolph came close—but we are still here. Now we are faced with the biggest crisis in our history—the wacko fundamentalist Islamic terrorists are out to eradicate and wipe Israel off the map. How do you fight a martyr-loving enemy that is dedicated to our obliteration? If someone is willing to die for their cause, it may be impossible to stop. Fuck them. Fuck 'em!

"Ferdinand and fucking Isabella said to the Jews, 'get the hell out of Spain.' Why? Well, in reality, it has been going on forever... 'Kill the Jews.' We were blamed for everything: bad luck, heartache, plague, poverty, and every motherfucking disaster that presented without basis or etiology. People were convinced that God would not have initiated a mass disaster or induced desolate poverty—so it must have been the Hellenic Jew bastards—couldn't have been any other reason. There was no other explanation.

"So, many of my ancestors left Spain. Most inhabitants of our town, our shtetl—which is now a park near Gava, just west of Barcelona—hid in the Pyrenees for several years. Eventually, they settled in this region. My immediate relatives purchased this property, farmed the fertile land, and cultivated successful mercantile businesses in nearby Marseille. Through all that, they raised their families with love and education and never wavered from their faith—my family—my faith."

"Some folks from Spain went to North Africa,

Caracas, Turkey, England, Russia, and other small communities on the continent—really a micro-story of the greater diaspora. Ironically, the Pyrenees were used for eons by every outlaw and warmonger to hide, wreak havoc, smuggle arms, and plan attacks. Ha... we were escaping from the fucking Germans who used the mountains to generate evil and promulgate destruction on everyone.

"We subsisted in Spain for 1400 years. There were times of tranquility and other times of hellish orgies as in 1013, when a group of fanatical Muslims massacred five thousand Jews. Through it all, our culture survived and even flourished. Maybe that's why we are so astonishingly resilient—they can torture us, maim us, and steal our treasures, but they can't kill our souls. Remember, we are 'the chosen'... ha, some great honor.

"That crazy cleft-lipped fucker wanted to bury Moses and the Ten Commandments—can you believe that? Well, fuck him—he's the one that's burning in Hell. My family was banished from the living, targeted for extermination just like ants and bees: squish 'em, burn 'em, and gas 'em. Fuck Hitler and all his motherfuckers.

"In the early thirties, everything started falling apart for European Jews. At first, most were in denial. 'How could this be,' they asked? 'How could this be? We are citizens of Poland, Belgium, Czechoslovakia, France, and the rest of the world.'

"Well, the rest of the world mollified the bastard—fucking appeased him. They gave the Fuhrer everything he wanted: factories, railroads, and countries. They gave him whole countries. The great conciliator, fucking Chamberlain, and his cronies acquiesced and sacrificed living people—they gave him the Jews.

"In the mid-thirties, anti-Semitic laws were decreed to keep Jews out of every profession: law, teaching, music, and even farming, and yet many Jews did not 'believe.'

"The rest is history."

Don't miss the next adventure in Cyprus... the mind-blowing sequel

to

Altered State of Affairs

with Steven, Avra, and Cindy

Coming soon...

www.ingramcontent.com/pod-product-compliance
Lightning Source LLC
Chambersburg PA
CBHW021140310726
48971CB00002B/415